BREAKING FREE

Alicia L. McCalla

Heart Ally Books
Camano Island, Washington

Published by:
Heart Ally Books
26910 92nd Ave NW C5-406, Stanwood, WA 98292
Published on Camano Island, WA, USA
www.heartallybooks.com

ISBN-13 (epub): 978-0-9835133-8-4
ISBN-13 (paperback): 978-0-9835133-7-7
Library of Congress Control Number: 2011945345

*To my grandfather,
Marshall Teague, the
inspiration behind
Breaking Free's holographic
"granddad."*

Acknowledgments

First of all, I'd like to thank God for giving my life purpose and a mission. I truly am humbled, grateful and I appreciate all that has been given to me. Next, I'd like to thank my great friend and publisher: Lisa Norman. Thank you Lisa, for being so helpful, caring, and supportive. Without you, I never would have been able to launch my writing career or publish *Breaking Free*.

I'd also like to thank my graphic designer, Eithne O'Hanlon, for creating such an awesome book cover. And I'd like to thank my marvelous editor, Valjeanne Jeffers, for her fabulous and fantastic content editing. I'd also like to thank the two men in my life: Howard and Asante McCalla. You two have endured more than any spouse and child should have to. I love you both, and sincerely appreciate your love, support, and help. You both are amazing!

I'm so grateful to my family members and friends who listened to me rattle on about publishing *Breaking Free*. I'd like to say thank you to: Connie Campbell, Lynda Cunningham, Valerie Nunn, Valerie Cunningham, Samara Etheridge, Kristina Nunn, Vershawn Young, Regina Hackett, Amber Jones, Margie Lawson, Sharon Cooper, and Delaney Diamond; for taking the time to help me make critical decisions.

I must also say thank you, to my wonderful writing community. There are so many of you that have helped me along the way; especially the members of the *Georgia Romance Writers* and *Romance Writers of America*. Without your nurturing support and kindness, I would not have had the courage to finish *Breaking Free* or publish it. I'd also like to thank the members of the *Black Science Fiction Society*, for their support and kindness.

Thanks so much, to everyone, who has supported and helped me further my writing career. I'm very grateful that you're a part of my life. *Muah!*

Prologue

"Genetically Enhanced Persons or GEPs are dangerous. As Humans United, we have to control these dangerous abominations. Every GEP must have the power reducing chip infused within their DNA. I just hope they never figure out the code to disabling the chip. For now, the Coalition to Assimilate Genetically Enhanced Persons— CAGE—can use it to keep them from taking over our world...."

—News Conference with the President of Humans United, June 2000

The betrayal ...

As Red Death jammed the IV needle into his arm, betrayal pierced his soul. Dr. Gary Leonard Kates, founder of the Revolution against CAGE, was tied to a chair. He thought about his three little granddaughters as the lethal serum pulsed through his veins. He refused to tell Red Death the code. He'd take the secret to his death.

The poisoned taste ignited inside his mouth, as her rose perfume suffocated him.

Everything about her disgusted him.

He hated the way she pranced around in her skin-tight, vinyl, red suit and spike heels. He could tell that she enjoyed torturing him, her former mentor. But what pissed him off more was that Brockman was watching.

"Dr. Kates, CAGE needs those codes," Red Death hissed, "more than your Revolution!"

His lungs burned. "How could I have selected *you* as my protégée?"

He turned from her as his voice trailed away. She'd been like a daughter to him, and Brockman like a son. Their betrayal only hastened the need for his martyrdom.

He refused to look at her and she grabbed his face, forcing him to meet her eyes. "I'm always saving your butt! Just like now!"

"You think mind-swiping me is the answer?" He hiccuped and coughed up mucus. "You think making me a puppet is worth the freedom of your own kind?"

Dr. Kates's veins caught fire—the flames spread from the bottom of his spirit to the top of his soul. Perspiration rolled down his graying beard, and he screeched out a spasm-distressed yell.

"Something's *wrong!*" Brockman shouted.

Red Death's spiked heels made panicked, clicking noises across the lab floor. She shook him. "What have you done, you old fool?"

"Double crosser! I hope your new CAGE job was worth it!" His voice scratchy with finality. "You *Judas!*" He watched Brockman shrink with the knowledge of his impending death.

Dr. Kates knew that he'd done the right thing. But regret washed over him. Chemicals from the mind-swipe procedure, intermingled with the suicide cocktail that he'd injected himself with. He'd done this before copying his consciousness into his computer.

Before tonight, the doctor would've trusted them with his secrets. But no more. He would leave most of them to his daughter, Dorothy, to pass on to his granddaughters. He'd told her about Red Death, but not about Brockman. She'd have to figure him out on her own.

Dr. Kates let out another seizure-filled scream. The lab chair crackled and crunched from his thrashing, the seat dark with his torrential sweating. His body doubled over with the effects of the lethal drugs. The restraints held him tight—so much so that he'd almost ripped himself free.

Red Death slapped him. "Calm down and tell me what you did so I can save you!"

He laughed, triumphant.

She slapped him again. "*Tell* me!"

"I'll never reveal my secrets to you!" the doctor spat. And he had so many.

He rolled his head from side to side. He saw Brockman sprint towards the door. Dr. Kates yelled behind him, "Come back here! Come *back!* Don't leave before...."

His genetically-enhanced abilities became feral, as the ache of his brain caving in continued. An uncontrollable whirlwind of objects and sounds crashed around him. Blood oozed from his eyes, nose and ears.

Red Death gazed into his eyes. She tried to use her touch telekinetic, GEP abilities to stop the reaction.

It was too late.

Her white face grew paler and sat in stark contrast to his dark skin. He smiled as her usually perfect blond hair swirled around her face in a maddened frenzy. She'd lost control. He watched a thin stream of blood dribble from her nose. It felt good to make her squirm.

"You stupid old man!" She shrank back from him, as objects banged and cracked around them from the wildness of his abilities.

Dr. Kates felt his consciousness slipping away. But he knew that the code was safe and tucked away ... later to be passed on to his super-enhanced granddaughters. They would become the weapons to avenge his untimely death.

He gave her an eerie, clairvoyant smile. With his last breath came a bloody, gurgled premonition, "My Revolution will destroy CAGE and crush you...."

Chapter 1

15 years later ...

"We take people in for questioning who are undeniably guilty. With our monitoring technology we know immediately that they've broken the law. GEPs must be dealt with severely."

—Dr. Herman Geiger, CAGE News Conference

I got to get to Mom! XJ Patterson made it to the open clearing in front of her home. She turned back to see her classmates on the school bus gawking at the backed-up traffic, and CAGE cars in front of her home.

They'd have more to gossip about now. XJ took a deep cleansing breath and shook off her aggravation. From her peripheral vision, she saw a CAGE officer the size of a football player barreling towards her. She didn't have time for this!

She gathered up her braids into a makeshift ponytail, and pulled out her audio stun gun. It was illegal for GEPs to use their abilities without CAGE permission, but not to carry weapons. They couldn't arrest her for having it.

The stench of burned flesh filled her nostrils. Her mother's bluish, electric light danced across the clearing ahead of her.

The burly, CAGE officer was nearly on top of her. "Offspring of Dorothy Kates-Patterson, cease or be reduced!"

XJ wanted to fight back to save time, but knew that using her abilities would get her in more trouble. So instead she shot him. He fell back and his body shuddered.

"I just wanna see my *mom!* Is that too much to ask?" She yelled at the other officers and rolled under a downed log for cover.

XJ felt a surge inside her mind. They were trying to activate the power-reducing mechanism but it wasn't working on her. The officers probably couldn't figure out why her abilities weren't diminished. They didn't know that her grandfather had embedded the code inside her DNA.

This was why everyone treated her so special, and why she detested her life. She closed her eyes and re-opened them. Broad shoulders came into view. She took a shot and stunned a blond, CAGE officer.

Her telekinetic abilities shuddered throughout her body. She was ready to fight! This was taking too long! Forget them finding out that their stupid, power-reducer didn't work on her. Now, her unhampered ability pushed adrenalin through her body and her world woke up.

"Launch the power reducer again!" XJ heard a Slavic accent through a nearby headset.

Behind him, she saw a branch wrapped in kudzu hanging from a tree. She focused her mind, and forced the branch to swing and smash into the CAGE officer's wide neck. It hit his kill switch. His brown eyes looked shocked as he buckled under the limb like a fallen giant.

Three down ... finally!

XJ raced across the clearing to where burned, aquatic-ability CAGE officers were fighting her pyrokinectic mother. Watching the battle, she started to worry.

Her mother was strong, but she couldn't hold out against them and their power reducer for much longer. XJ didn't know what to do. She didn't want to disturb mom's concentration but she had to do *something*.

I got to help her! She telepathically opened her side of the parent-child mind link, creating a safe time bubble for them to talk.

Mom, what's going on?

Her mother turned to focus on her, and fully opened the link. *XJ!*

Time froze. Wind, sound, trees, CAGE officers—all danced to a slow motion beat. Her heart thumped weirdly until she gazed into the face of her mother. Her mom embraced her and XJ felt a sense of warmth, belonging and comfort.

Dorothy looked battle-fatigued and dirty. But XJ could still see her beautiful brick-tone red and brown sugar complexion peaking through the grime. Her mother's wine colored dreadlocks hung down her back in a spiral-curled pattern.

Looking at her, dressed only in cargo Capri pants, yellow tee-shirt and flowered flip flops; it was hard for XJ to imagine her as anything but a normal mom. She certainly didn't look like a die-hard revolutionary. Her mother's height made her look more like a retired super model with a generous, earthy beauty.

"Mom, what's happening?! Why are you fighting them?"

Dorothy pushed her braids out of her eyes. "I broke the law and they're here to take me away."

"What? Why? What did you do?" Worry framed XJ's words.

Her mother cleared her throat. "Our family made sacrifices for the freedom of all GEPs. This time, to protect us all, I'm sacrificing myself. It's the only way."

XJ's stomach squeezed with pain. "No! Mom—*no!* Why do you have to sacrifice yourself to this stupid war! I *need* you! Why can't we live a normal life? Can you take back what you've done?"

Time swirled faster.

Her mother's stare felt distant.

"You must fulfill your grandfather's mission. You must become a revolutionary. You're our last hope. Your generation must carry on where ours ends."

Tears burst from XJ's eyes as she gripped her mother. "Will you stop with the babble? All my life you talked about my destiny and our family's legacy! I'm only *17 years old!* I *need* you!"

Her mother breathed deeply and cupped XJ's face. "Oh, child, you are so much more! You're our reason, hope, and joy! You stand on the backs of many! You must take up the fight, and save our people from their oppression. It's up to you now."

XJ tried to push through confusion and chaos in her soul. She wanted all of this to go away. She wanted a normal, teenage life.

"Bull!" she shouted. "It's crap trying to live up to the legacy of dead people! I'm sorry granddad was murdered! I'm sorry that GEPs are second-class citizens. I'm sorry Daddy left you for that blond, black widow and her stepford daughter! I'm sorry—!"

"I can't hold the time bubble. You must work with the Revolution. Find Brockman ... here...." Her mom thrust something into her hand.

"Brockman? I don't trust him. I don't know why you do. What's this?" XJ fumbled with the odd shaped ruby ring Dorothy pushed in her hand. It had a platinum band and was encrusted with diamonds.

"It's a family heirloom. I didn't want them to take me away until I gave it to you. When everyone leaves, go inside the house and put it on. I have to go. I love you."

Her mother kissed her forehead and time sucked her back into the electric firefight.

"No! Mom! No!" XJ screamed until it felt her lungs would explode.

Suddenly, her mother was embroiled in battle again. XJ slipped the ring into her jacket pocket and looked on in horror.

Chapter 2

"Brandon Miller and Heather Stillwater are perfect together. They have the pedigree, complimentary GEP abilities and perfect looks. They're on the rise together."

—GEP Network's Teen Sensation, Talk Show Host

"What the hell?" Brandon Miller stumbled back from the opening of the men's room door. He was trying to escape Heather, and the rest of his father's butt kissers at the GEP Network Banquet.

"What's more important than me?" Heather swung her blond hair, and screamed as she barged in; locking the door behind her. "Is there someone else?"

Brandon let out a heavy, irritated breath. "Of course, there's someone *much* better than you," he said sarcastically.

Heather walked up to him until they were eye-to-eye, then stopped. She smelled like roses. Brandon had to admit, the girl was hot. She had blue eyes, gorgeous blond curls and a curvy body. His eyes roamed over her frame and settled on her breasts.

He took a deep breath. None of it was worth dealing with her freaky, stalker personality.

He watched her eyes linger on his chest. "Let's get back together," she breathed. "I know what you like."

Brandon felt his temperature rise, as Heather grabbed his hand and guided him towards the men's stall.

He remembered how well she did that thing with her mouth, in the boy's bathroom at school. It had been worth the three days of In-School Suspension.

Two years ago, he would've given anything for her tongue on his manhood. But now, he was sick of her theatrics.

Undeterred, she pushed closer. "I *know* you want me." Heather pulled his hand up towards her lips, then rubbed it against her tanned breasts.

He yanked his hand away. "I'm not interested in what you're offering." The flat, emotionless words flew from his mouth.

Brandon gripped the sides of the sink—trying to grab hold of something real. He looked at his reflection in the mirror above the sink, and his mind went back to Revolution TV ... and XJ.

XJ Patterson, Heather's step sister, and the granddaughter of Dr. Gary Leonard Kates.... There were so many reasons for him to stay away from XJ. But so many more reasons why he wanted her. For one, she was gorgeous. XJ's brown skin, curvy shape, and exotic hair turned him on....

He felt Heather massaging his back. That wouldn't work today.

"Don't you get that I don't want you?" Brandon gave an exasperated grumble and turned to face her.

Her heels clicked on the tiled floor, as she shoved her body closer to his. "You'll want me soon enough. I'm the only one that's a suitable mate."

"Haven't you looked at the news today?" Brandon growled. "XJ and her mother are in trouble!"

"You think I care about my stupid, jungle bunny, step sister and her lunatic mother? *Please!*" She tossed her blond curls and started rubbing him again. "We're the next GEP power couple. We're the same mate-designation type. We're perfect together. You *can't* say no."

Brandon moved back. "I'd rather go to jail than be your designated mate!"

Heather went Scarlet O'Crazy. "Brandon, we've *got* to be together!" She crooned and whined in a tone that sounded like nails on a chalkboard. "I've already told my friends that you'd escort me to the Miss GEP High School Pageant! It's *televised!*"

Someone knocked on the door.

Brandon's jaw tightened. "I'm not gonna be your escort!"

Heather's voice cracked, her eyes widened and he saw a tick in the corner of her mouth. "Don't you understand how *important* this is to me?"

His eyes narrowed as they met hers. "I don't care."

"You're mine!" Heather's nostrils flared and a growl slipped from her throat. "Can't you see that?"

Brandon whipped around to turn his back to her, and Heather stumbled off balance. Concerned knocks assaulted the door. "Is everything okay?" a voice called.

Brandon raked his hands through his hair. He thought about his mom. Her warm healing smile, caring green eyes and her delicate scent of lavender. And then, the memory he'd repressed flooded him: his mother lying in a pool of blood, and a CAGE officer wiping his k-bar clean.

Things were different before. He'd agreed to go on the *Teen Sensation* TV show his father bankrolled before her death. But after her murder, he grew angry because his dad refused to search for his mother's killer. Everything changed and he no longer wanted the same life.

He fast forwarded to Heather's crazed phone calls in the middle of the night, and the constant threats. Before his mother's murder, Heather was all he wanted.

Now he wanted to be done with her and his old life.

Brandon wanted to show the world that he was more than a rich, technopathic GEP brat. He wanted to be more than Todd Miller's "son." He wanted to help someone besides himself.

Above all he wanted to further the Revolution. And he had a plan.

Brandon gave Heather a nasty grin and shrugged. "You need to take one of your little, white nerve pills. 'Cause I wouldn't take you to Burger Palace."

Heather shot him a scheming smile. *"Don't!* Don't touch me like *that!"* She screamed, savagely ripping her form-fitting, hot pink dress. She puckered her lips and blew him a black widow's loving kiss.

Furious knocks and bangs assaulted the other side of the door. Brandon sauntered over and unbolted the lock. His father marched in to assess the situation, while Brandon stood back, crossed his arms and scowled.

He truly despised his father.

"Son, what's going on?" Todd looked from him to Heather.

Brandon hated that he looked so much like his father. He hated Todd's big shoulders, blue eyes, blond hair and commanding presence. It made him feel good that at six foot four, he towered over his dad, but everything else made him feel inferior and angry.

Heather hung her head low, and sobbed like a wounded animal. Her mother, Nadia, pushed into the men's room. Brandon despised her, too. She was a phony and full of it. Brandon folded his arms tighter across his chest, and wrinkled his nose: still frowning.

"Oh sweetie, what happened? Are you okay?" Nadia's perfect, blond curls bounced as she turned towards Brandon, and gave him an accusing scowl.

Brandon pursed his lips and ground his teeth, while Heather spurted out her story. He knew the female brigade would win. No one would listen to him. At least this time, it would turn out in his favor.

His dad turned around and frowned. "Is this true?"

Todd could be such a dick sometimes. *Would it hurt him to take my side, just once?*

Brandon narrowed his eyes. "Of course it's not true! But what does it matter? You've decided that she's telling the truth! Never mind that she tried to rape me!"

"That's *enough!"* Todd waved his arms, already losing composure. Brandon chuckled inwardly. At least his father, the GEP Television Mogul, was showing some guts.

Brandon saw Nadia's face flush. Her expression was unreadable as she pulled Heather's crying face closer, "She's like three-fourths your size! I can't believe you'd say such things about my daughter!"

Heather lifted her face. It was tracked with lying tears and her eyes told a fake tale. Brandon smirked.

His dad turned with unexpected ferocity. "I can't believe you'd do something like this!"

Brandon squared his shoulders and hit his fist into his hand. "I *told* you the truth! She tried to hurt me!"

Witness's eyes peered greedily through the door of the bathroom. This little squabble had the potential to make it on gossip news. Bad press was a bad idea for the owner of GEP TV.

Brandon watched Todd shrink back and fold his arms. "Let's not discuss this now. I've got business to take care of."

His father had no balls when his media flunkies were around. Brandon turned his back on him, dismissing him. "That's fine dad. I've got business, too."

Brandon forced his way through Todd's media butt kissers, and headed towards the elevator.

He relaxed his shoulders. His plan to escape worked. On the way out the door, he saw Heather as she glanced up through her manipulative tears. Brandon gave her a "cat that ate the canary" smile, and boarded the elevator.

In the garage he leapt into his convertible red and black Mustang. He relaxed back into the bucket-control seat, and used his technopathic ability to meld with his baby. The car shot off.

He patted the console. He had everything he needed to broadcast an episode of Revolution TV. He hoped he could convince XJ to tell her family's story. But more than that, he hoped that he could get close enough to her so she'd be his girlfriend.

He swore under his breath that he wouldn't be a slave to the network, like his dad. *I'm gonna tell people the truth about CAGE and the GEP Revolution.*

Chapter 3

"This is Brandon Miller, your hardworking reporter. I'm here at the home of Revolutionary Dorothy Kates-Patterson, where there's a showdown between her and CAGE. Does CAGE really need 20 officers to take down one woman? It's insane! More details to follow!"

—Breaking news, Revolution TV

Hide, sweetie, hide! She heard her mother inside her head.

No. I want to help! XJ pulled out her gun. She was ready to shoot.

Her mother's power heated the gun metal and she dropped it.

Not yet. Soon. Her mom said telepathically. *You'll accomplish nothing if you get in this battle. Hide!*

XJ tried to send her mother another message but the link closed. She grappled with her confused anxiety. She found a small section of short trees and kneeled down to peer through an opening.
The fight moved back and forth like a tennis match. The water-ability officers closed in with a mixture of hail, ice and salt water to combat the electric fire streaming from her mother's fingers.

As the officers drew closer, her mother took another one down. XJ wondered how long her mom could hold on. The odds felt impossible. She inched closer and stuck her head further out. One of the officers saw her and moved with lightening speed.

She froze with terror. She heard her mother screaming, but all her awareness was focused on the face of death. Finally, her survival instincts kicked-in and she took off running—scratching and scrubbing her legs on the bush. She turned back to look for her mother.

Red and blue, electric fire balls flew from her mother's hands in frenzied motion. Her mother was trying to save her.

XJ slid and squeezed underneath a large, downed tree into what she thought was a safe place. The officer stopped, his face still. He seemed to be participating in a hive-like telepathic communication. She rolled flat on her belly into a prone position. She tried to focus her telekinetic ability like a sniper rifle, but nothing happened.

Her power was spent.

The young woman breathed slowly, trying to figure out what to do. Her mother had told her to hide and now she had exposed both of them! She felt stupid. He shifted his legs and headed for her.

XJ rolled out and dashed to the opposite side of her house. If she could make it into the neighbor's yard, she'd get away. Her legs pumped harder. As she reached the clearing a cold caress from the officer's water ability rushed up her leg and dragged her down.

She fell—shaking from the biting cold. The arctic frost inched up her thighs. She faintly heard her mother screaming as the frozen, cold water spread over her.

Her teeth chattered. She looked up at the pale, white CAGE officer. "I—Is T—T—his H—H—ow Y—Y—ou G—G—Get your kicks from freez—zing a k—k—id?"

The CAGE officer smiled a nightmarish grin, as the icy water continued to drown her shirt and jeans.

XJ's body convulsed. Her skin turned a chilly, midnight shade of blue. Hypothermia loomed. She'd lost feeling in her legs and arms. And she was *scared*. She turned her head to see her mother still furiously fighting.

A voice over a loud speaker said, "Stand down Dorothy Kates-Patterson or we will freeze your offspring to death!"

XJ whispered frosty breath, "Bastards...!" before the unmanageable cold forced her insides to do the shakes. Her eyes froze shut. She'd let her mother down and now she was going to die a frozen mess.

Suddenly, her body warmed. Her eyes popped back open and she saw blue fire shoot from each of her mother's hands: one to warm her and the other to scorch the backs of the officers. Her mother had called forth a maternal wrath that sent charred flesh flying. Soon, no one stood in her mother's path. Once Dorothy saw that XJ was warm and safe, she collapsed.

XJ's body was thawing and moving slowly. She yelled within her mind. *Mom, get up! Get up!*

She realized that there were more CAGE officers coming to finish them. In a moment of clarity, her eyes met her mother's.

Her mom mouthed, *I love you.* And then she turned into an electric, fire bomb that seared everything except XJ.

Panicked, she rolled over still sluggish. Her mind readjusted. Nothing moved including her mother. Silence ensued. Seared and singed bodies lay motionless in the yard. The smell made her sick, but she was more worried about her mother. She crawled to her mother and tried to get up. Her body was still weak.

She crashed back to the ground. *She had to get to her Mom!* That's when she heard someone screaming and realized it was her own voice. "Mom! *Mom!* Answer *me!*"

XJ squeezed her eyes shut. Tears flowed down her cheeks. Her teeth ground into her bottom lip. A strong metallic taste filled her mouth. Her stomach lurched. She opened her eyes to the backyard battle zone. She knew that she should feel pain, but her mind was focused on her mother's still form. She tried to stand, dizziness smashed her back to her knees. But she would not be deterred.

She stood with strength of mind, and walked towards her mother.

Male arms engulfed her and pulled her back.

"No!" Her voice sounded foreign, hoarse. "I've got to get to my mom!" She tried to push pass the soft barrier. Her face found his chest.... He smelled good. She let his warmth soothe her.

His muffled voice consoled her, "It's too dangerous. CAGE is everywhere. Let's get you out of here. Your mother wouldn't want you in the middle of this."

Slowly, XJ's sanity crept back to her. With her eyes closed, she took a deep breath. She heard mechanical swoosh and thumping noises moving closer ... and closer.

What the heck is that?

XJ's eyes popped open, and she whipped her head around when she realized what it was. She watched as a pack of CAGE officers funneled down from a black helicopter. Her stomach tensed. She tried to pull away from the strong arms and run to her mom but he held her. His strong arms covered and protected her from the scene.

But she could still peek through. The CAGE officers pulled out black handguns and opened fire on her mother's still form. She couldn't catch her breath.

Her eyes widened and she screamed, "Oh *God!* They're *killing* her!" XJ collapsed into his arms ... deep, heavy sobs followed.

"It's just tranqs." The voice soothed her. "They've only tranquilized her."

Her mind stilled and her mother's faded whisper telepathically filled her mind. *I love you. Don't worry about my sacrifice. Focus on your mission. Free GEPs forever.*

The link snapped shut.

XJ closed her eyes and her body relaxed against the man. She heard tires crunch on the gravel up her driveway and come to a squeaky stop. Her eyes opened again and a large, black vehicle blocked her view.

She took off and this time almost reached her mother, but stumbled and skidded down on the ground.

The male arms pulled her back up, hugging her from behind. *"No!* It's too dangerous!"

Spent, XJ watched as CAGE officers dispassionately threw her mother's fallen form into the backseat of the vehicle. Her shoulders slumped and broke down again.

The gentle arms held her tight while she sobbed.

Chapter 4

"This is Blake Cooper, reporting from the home of Dorothy Kates-Patterson. It appears that CAGE has pulled no stops in subduing her! This is a battle zone!"
—Breaking News, GEP Network News

Brandon held XJ close. He stroked her braided hair. The texture and consistency felt different from his, but he liked it. He liked her brown skin too.

"Shh ... It's okay. I'm so sorry." He could sense her vulnerability and his heart went out to her. Something deep inside wanted to protect her—to care for her; to make sure she was alright.

XJ seemed defenseless—helpless—as he rocked them both back and forth. He realized that she was a couple of inches shorter than him and fit comfortably in his arms. He took a deep breath and smelled the soft scent of strawberries.

Tenderness and empathy washed over him. He had no idea how he would help her, but he would find a way. Her sobs subsided and he gazed into her eyes. Deep compassion and heartfelt warmth flowed between them.

"Brandon? Brandon Miller?" XJ pulled out of his embrace.

He lost his ability to speak for a moment. He knew he'd come to see about her. Since the summer, he'd come to love XJ more and more. But he knew he messed up and he wanted to fix it.

He couldn't tell her that. "I—I was coming to see if you needed help...." He stuttered. He wanted to touch her hand and pull her back into the embrace.

"I don't need any help from you." XJ crossed her arms and narrowed her eyes. Although she was only a few inches away, it seemed like a wall was erecting between them. Brandon didn't want that.

He cleared his throat. "Well, I finally started Revolution TV and I came to get the story. But when I saw...."

"You're here to get a *story?*" He could see the hurt on XJ's face.

He wanted to tell her that he was here for *her;* that he was sorry about what happened before. He wanted to tell her that he'd made a mistake, choosing Heather over her. But now it seemed too late.

"I just thought that I could get the exclusive and...." Brandon's heart pumped faster. He was losing her, again! How could he be so *stupid?* He just wanted to get closer to her.

"Are you kidding me?" XJ blew out her breath and pointed her finger at him. "You just don't change do you? Always concerned about what's in your best interest!"

"I just wanna help.... Let me use my influence to help you." He reached out to touch her face.

XJ dodged his touch and moved back. "Don't you ever get tired of using your dad's money and power for your own benefit? Don't you get tired of trying to use other people for your own purposes?"

Brandon saw a camera flash in his peripheral vision. This would be all over the news. His stomach somersaulted. Should he care? A match between him and XJ was illegal. But he knew other GEP's dated outside of their mate-designation type all the time.

I wanna tell her it doesn't matter, but it does! He shouldn't be seen with her in public until he could figure out how to use Revolution TV to change this.

XJ continued to let him have it. "I just watched my mother almost *die!* What do you really want?"

"I just want to work with you to tell your story on Revolution TV. I think I can help change perceptions and put pressure on the government to...."

"You're asking me if I'll be your paparazzi gossip for the day?" XJ waved her hands in fury. "How dare you try to use me like that!"

Reporters started to fill out along the tree line and cameras flashed like crazy. This wasn't going the way Brandon planned at all.

He lowered his voice. "I know that we had some issues. I was thinking that we could join together and...."

XJ yelled at him. "I don't want to have *anything* to do with you! Aren't you still dating my uppity, white step sister? Isn't *that* enough gossip for you?"

Brandon watched XJ storm off.

He rubbed the back of his neck, as he saw her frantically march to the porch while cameras flashed. How could he convince her to work with him? If he could figure out a way to use Revolution TV to help change things, maybe they could be together.

But she's not making it easy.

Chapter 5

"I'm ready for the Miss GEP High School Pageant! You already know who'll be my escort. Brandon Miller, the love of my life."

—Heather Stillwater, GEP Network's Teen Sensation

Heather could care less that Brandon left. She was sick of tracking ... or rather dating him. She clenched her jaw and put her hand behind her head.

Which one is it?

She always had two people inside her head, and she never knew who would take over. This person, though, felt calm. Real. She felt her best when this Heather took over. She smiled to herself. She wanted to be free from all the drama. She wanted to have some fun—to get away.

She wanted to see Saskia.

Heather rounded the corner to the ladies room. She was going to change her clothes and hang out with Saskia at the skating rink. She'd already texted her. Her heart skipped a beat. She could feel her face flush. This was exactly what she needed, some time away from everything—especially Brandon. He didn't like her anyway.

Her head hurt. Her hands shook. Not again. Her other personality screamed, railed, yelled in her head. *Brandon does love me! Let me out! I've got to find him!*

The Heather in control laughed out loud. "He hates you. You're only doing this to humor her. And mother doesn't care about you either."

You're wrong. Mother loves me. She takes care of me. She's good to me. The other voice inside her, blathered on and on and on.

"I'm not buying it. I'm in control and you can't have it back. Look how you've messed up our lives."

Heather pushed the door open to the ladies room. Someone shoved her away from the door in the opposite direction. She lost her grip on her gym bag, and it fell to the floor.

Heather's mother grabbed her arm and dragged her into a nearby corner. "Why did you let him get away?" Nadia's blue eyes pierced her soul.

Heather shrank back as far as she could. She took in a quick breath.

That's when her two minds began to fight.

One side screamed, *Don't do what she wants! She's just using you!*

A second voice whined, *Do what she wants! She'll reward you later!*

Heather's body shook. She needed the medicine—there were too many voices and sensations, too many thoughts. Heather bit down on her lip and swallowed. Couldn't she just hang out with Saskia? Everything would be better and she'd be able to think clearly.

Her mother shook her and looked around to make sure no one was watching. *"Answer me!"* Nadia was focused on her like a laser. Heather widened her eyes.

"I—I don't know. Brandon's sneaky that way." Heather felt cold sweat run down her back. The two voices warred inside her mind like a clash of the titans. They talked so fast she couldn't catch up. She just wanted them both to be quiet.

"Shut-up!" She screamed. Her body wouldn't stop shaking. She couldn't get herself together. She trembled.

Her mother looked into her eyes and hissed, "Who are you? *Which* one?"

"I *hate* you!" Heather spat. "Get your hands off me!"

Her mother's lip curled. "You *will* do what I want."

Heather knew what was coming. She had to get away. Her calm mind needed to stay in control. She didn't want to do it. She didn't want to do any of it. All those horrible things her mother made her do. She wanted to run.

"Why can't you leave me alone? Why can't I do what I want for a change? Why can't you let me be who I am?" Heather tried to wriggle away from her mother.

Her mother had her stapled against the wall with her forearm while she took off her red glove. She went straight for Heather's neck and held it with an iron grip. Her mother's touch telekinesis pulsed through her entire body like a blooming, hot flower. Real tears gushed. She wanted to scream but knew the consequences so she suffered the searing pain.

Her two minds quieted. Both were clear. They had to do what her mother wanted to stop this pain.

"I'm sorry, mother. I'll find Brandon." Heather choked back tears and let her shoulders deflate. The pain burned everywhere, crippling her. Saskia would have to wait. The disappointment burned, too.

"Please! I won't disobey you again!" The real Heather faded into the background.

"I'm glad we understand each other." The pain receded and Heather felt Nadia's other ability flood her. It was intense calm and comfort ... a warm and loving sense of security. She relaxed into this feeling. It was like a drug. Heather felt high and her mind was clear.

She collapsed onto her mother. "I'm sorry. I didn't mean it. I'll do whatever you want."

Nadia rubbed her daughter's hair, then pushed her back against the wall, her eyes determined. "Now, you *find* that Miller boy. And don't let him out of your sight."

This Heather was happy to do whatever her mother wanted. This Heather enjoyed it. This Heather smiled. Spending time with Saskia was a fleeting dream. She would do whatever she could to make her mother happy.

And she would do whatever it took, to make sure that Brandon was hers for good.

Chapter 6

"Brandon and I may as well be soul mates. We are compatible mate-designation types."
—Heather Stillwater, GEP Network's Teen Sensation

"Brandon, it's Heather. Pick-up." Heather snapped the phone shut. She hated that Brandon had gotten away. Pissed, she dialed again and again ... and again.

"Ugh!" She said out loud and shoved each one of her legs into her hot-pink jeans. She zipped up her pants ... then stopped.

Her hands trembled. She took out the little white pills that her mom gave her and popped three more in her mouth. Nadia told her the pills helped calm her down so she could focus.

Brandon wouldn't get far.

Heather bent over to put on her chunky, pink, combat boots.

"I know I can find him." She muttered to herself. She was *so* glad the other voice was silent. "Finally, I'm alone."

She stood up and warm arms encircled her from behind. Warm, inviting, tender, and caring. They could only belong to one person.

Heather smiled from cheek to cheek, "Brandon! I knew you'd come back!"

She whipped around and faced Saskia. *"You!"*

Saskia released her. "Hey, you ready?" She always asked in such a kind way.

Heather didn't need this. She had to get rid of her. "No. I'm not going anywhere with you."

Heather turned her back on Saskia but could still see her in the mirror.

"Oh, you're busy, I get it." Her friend's brown eyes looked sad. Heather felt her other self wake up but she pushed her back into the abyss. She couldn't afford this distraction.

Heather sensed Saskia using her ability. She switched around and pointed her finger. "Don't even think about using that emotional, empathic crap on me."

The other Heather stirred. Saskia was a Slavic beauty. Heather loved her short brown hair, flawless skin, and freckled nose. She loved her generous face too.

The other voice inside her head tried to take over. *Just give me a minute!*

No. It's too dangerous.

Let me talk to her! Heather wiped her face with her hands. *You're not coming out!* Had she said that out loud? She couldn't tell. Her hands shook and her stomach churned.

"Shut up!" Heather tried to ignore everything going on inside. She pulled her pink turtle neck out of her bag and forced it on over her body. She'd pushed her head through and Saskia leaned over to kiss her cheek.

Heather shrank from her. "Back off!"

The other voice thrashed in conflict. Heather stepped back, bent over, and grabbed her head. She was drowning inside her own mind. Her heart pumped faster—she couldn't catch her breath. The meltdown slithered into her soul. She tried to stop it, but waves of confusion and frustration washed over her. The internal conflict was beating her up.

Saskia's warmth flooded her body. The soothing voice echoed throughout the room, centering her. "I'm here if you need me."

She could feel Saskia bringing her back, but it was the wrong personality.

Heather rocked on her heels and screamed, "You *can't* come out!" She straightened up and peered into the young woman's eyes. Sweat poured down her spine. "Go away," she said coldly. "You're distracting me."

She could feel her friend searching for the other Heather, but she'd forced her down. Heather's blood pumped a little slower. She took a deep breath.

"I understand." Saskia said in a small voice. "Maybe we can hang out later."

Heather's other mind knew she couldn't afford this right now. She skirted past Saskia and stopped in front of the mirror. She looked a mess so she whipped out her make-up and freshened up. She heard the door click behind her and knew that the woman was gone. She caught herself taking big gulps of air but she calmed down.

The other one couldn't come out. Not now.

"Brandon is all that matters." She told herself in the mirror as she smooched her lips together to put on her lipstick. "I've got to focus on what's important." Heather tapped into the preternatural part of herself.

Heather's body quieted, heating up as she used her GEP tracking ability and focused. Using her ability felt right. It was like sliding on a perfect pair of gloves. Her vision turned red.

She fixated on her target. *Brandon's just confused. He really adores and worships me. He just needs some help.*

She found him. Her abilities bloomed. She received a full image and instinctively knew how to track him down. Her whole body was drawn to his location. She mindlessly finished lacing up her boots and went to the garage to get into her hot-pink convertible Lexus. Her internal map helped her envision Brandon. She drove on, entranced but capable of following traffic laws.

Heather pulled up next to Brandon's car. She recognized this location as the *bad* part of town. She swiveled her head from side to side to investigate.

Wait … I know this yard. It belonged to her step sister.

Someone was sending her a text. Heather picked up her phone, scrolled down and saw it was Saskia. She blew out her breath impatiently.

She typed back, *Can't talk now. Trying to follow Brandon.*

Saskia texted, *Be careful, love.*

Something about Saskia made Heather calm. Feeling more confident, she stepped out onto the muddy sidewalk.

"Eww!" Heather shrieked, as she caught a stench of something that smelled like fried skunk.

She redialed Brandon. He didn't answer. How dare he treat her with such disrespect! Her hands shook. She needed another pill to calm her down. She popped another one.

Heather tramped through the sludge, downed trees and disgusting odor to find Brandon. With the smoke and the bright lights it was hard for her to see him, but her internal tracking kept her focused on him. He was the love of her life.

Heather heard muffled voices and hunkered behind a bush. The smoldering scene overwhelmed her until she saw Brandon's beautiful, tanned skin and spiky, blond hair. Her heart jumped. She would change his mind. She would *make* him adore and love her.

He must love…. Heather did a double take. She pulled her hair back in a ponytail with a hairclip and squinted.

Brandon held her black, step sister like he cared about her! She'd rip the little slut's eyes out! A fanatical growl escaped her lips. She shoved the top of her fist into her mouth and held the sound back.

Why the hell would Brandon leave me for that trash? XJ doesn't have my money, connections or mate-designation type! My step father chose pedigree over her mother.

Brandon would certainly pick *her* over XJ.

Heather scanned the area. She made out camera flashes and a crowd heading towards XJ. Heather would have to fix her step sister.   A plan formed inside her mind. She noticed a reporter in a hideous, trench coat and smiled. She'd recognized him as one of Nadia's stooges. Between this reporter and one of her mother's social workers, her step sister wouldn't stand a chance.

Chapter 7

"The Kates family have sacrificed everything for the freedom of GEPs but who's sacrificed for them?"
—John Brockman, Revolutionary News Conference

XJ couldn't believe that she'd just balled up in Brandon's jacket and then stomped away. Not only was he the richest, sexiest guy in school, but he was her step sister's long-time boyfriend. He smelled like fine cologne and he had a body out of this world.

She couldn't believe how gentle he'd treated her. But as sexy as he was on the outside, she couldn't be bothered with him. He'd already shown her what he thought of her at the wedding; and he'd chosen her step sister over her.

XJ could totally understand. They weren't the same mate-designation type. Nothing could ever come of their relationship. He couldn't add to his father's media fortune if he chose her.

She kept walking and refused to look back. A part of her wished that things were different. A part of her wanted the lives of GEPs to be free, so they could choose to love who they wanted.

She pulled her phone out and called her father. Since her dad married his mate-designation type, things were better for him financially. He now worked for a company that allowed him to use his transporter abilities.

He was somewhere in South America working on a short assignment. His new wife had helped him get the job. XJ's stomach turned when she thought of her step mother. Nadia Stillwater was the perfect wife—and the complete opposite of her mother.

"Dad, I need you! Mom's in trouble! CAGE has taken her away! Please come home!" XJ ended the voice message and slid her phone into her pocket. She still wished that her parents would get back together, but that wasn't going to happen.

She kept marching toward her front porch. Within minutes, the vultures with cameras exploded: they flashed, clicked, and blinded her. But she kept her head up and continued walking. XJ ripped CAGE's written, extraction order off the door, and turned towards the hungry reporters.

She took a deep, cleansing breath. This was her life. Always in the public spotlight. Always in front of carnivorous reporters. Always defending her family's name. She was so sick of it! Would she ever be a regular person?

She looked out on the sea of reporters in her backyard. Cameras flashed faster. The effect was dizzying but she put on her mask. It was the mask of the daughter of a revolutionary and the granddaughter of a martyr. Dorothy taught her to look straight ahead, stand tall, and be clear.

XJ's voice croaked a little, but came out strong, "As you can see, my mother has been taken away. My family needs time to deal with this. I'd like you all to leave."

Voices bombarded her. "XJ, did CAGE take your mother away because of her decision to sabotage your father and step mother's wedding?"

Her stomach churned. That wedding wouldn't go away! "My mom had nothing to do with that!" She let her anger settle and kept her composure.

Another voice boomed, "Is your mother guilty of building an army to take over humanity?"

XJ's back tightened. The rage boiled up, but she remained outwardly calm. "I won't dignify that with a response."

A female voice came next. "Your family has suffered so much with the assassination of your grandfather and now the arrest of your mother. What will you do?"

XJ let the question roll around in her head. She wanted to say that she was 17 years old and her mother was all she had. She wanted to say that she felt like breaking down. She bit her lip. Suddenly the cameras parted like an ocean, to allow a CAGE officer to march up to her. The fear freaked her out but she held fast. Cameras flashed even brighter. She stood her ground.

She didn't think he would harm her. And she was right. He had paperwork for her. Her chest pounded as she took it. The CAGE officer turned and pushed back through the crowd.

The papers said that her house had been confiscated as evidence. Her mother would receive the mind swipe procedure; and for her to pack her belongings, because she would be taken to a Zone 6 CAGE facility by a social worker within the hour.

XJ wanted to scream, but she kept her emotions in check. She needed these vultures on her side. "If I can prove that my mother is innocent and CAGE has acted falsely, who will tell the real story? Who will stand up with me against CAGE?"

The reporters gasped. They all knew what it meant to take on CAGE. Certainly torture, death or mind swiping. Silence ensued.

"I'll run your story!" all eyes shifted towards the voice. XJ looked into Brandon's determined eyes.

Her chest warmed with the thought of him helping her. But this was too dangerous for him. She needed one of the mainstream reporters to do this.

XJ glared at the crowd of reporters. "Not one of you will tell the truth? Why am I not surprised?" She turned her back on them and opened her front door.

"I'll do it." She heard a scratchy, male voice and turned to see who it belonged to.

She peered out. "Who's that?"

A scruffy looking, white man put away his notepad and took a puff of the cigarette hanging from his lips. "Finnegan Fitch."

"Dude, did you not get the memo that smoking kills?"

The reporters laughed nervously. XJ watched Fitch drop his cigarette and ground it out with his foot. He wore a tan trench coat; a dirty white, long-sleeve shirt; dark blue, worn-out dockers and a pair of funny looking loafers. XJ was not impressed.

"I'll run your story, kid." Fitch walked up to her and handed her his card.

Brandon jumped between them. "She doesn't need your card! I'm taking this story!"

XJ took the card and ignored Brandon. "You're willing to print the truth?"

Fitch smiled. "You get a chance to tell your side of the story. I'll make sure of that."

She thought about this. Her eyes wandered towards Brandon. His eyes silently said, *No*.

"Can you help me get my mom free?"

Brandon moved closer to XJ. "Don't listen to this bum. You can't trust him. Revolution TV can help...."

The reporter continued. "Well, that might be more difficult."

"Then no deal, go back with the rest of—" XJ's emotions swirled inside her. *I thought he could help!*

"Hold on! If you can prove that your mom is innocent, I can guarantee that the world knows it. I'll even pay you for the scoop. It's just...." Fitch touched his nose, avoiding eye contact with her.

"Just *what?*" She leaned forward.

"No, this isn't right!" Brandon shouted. *"I'll* tell your story. Revolution TV will help you! You don't have to—!"

The reporter cleared his throat and gave an awkward smile. "I've got to have whatever you find exclusively. No poachers. My articles carry a lot of weight and I'm sure we'll be able to free your mom."

XJ felt relief. She wanted all the reporters gone. She wanted her life back to normal. She wanted her mom back. She glanced at Brandon and more emotions surged through her.

"If I find anything, it's yours first! Now get rid of these people!" She pointed at the other reporters.

"That's all I needed to hear." Fitch turned away from her, and began clearing out the other reporters.

XJ turned toward Brandon. He looked crushed. *But he doesn't understand. I want these people gone. I want my mom to be free.*

Besides, he'd already chosen Heather at the wedding. He wasn't interested in her. Not really. She fidgeted with the card from Fitch.

Had she just made a deal with Satan or was Fitch her answer?

Chapter 8

"We don't know because we refuse to accept the truth.
Ignorance is dangerous in these troubled times."
—Dr. Gary Leonard Kates, Press Conference

Brandon recognized Fitch from his dad's newspaper division. He'd never liked Fitch. Something about him wasn't right and Brandon knew he had to prove it. He wiped sweat from his forehead. Even though it was spring, the Georgia heat still warmed him.

He watched in horror as XJ sealed the deal with Fitch. His stomach twisted in knots and he looked away. CAGE had removed all the corpses, but he could still smell the charred bodies. He couldn't understand why she'd done it. It made him mad.

All at once, his emotions softened. XJ was beautiful, confident, and lovely. He wanted to protect her. It pissed him off that she'd chosen Fitch over him. Brandon clenched his hands into stiff fists. His cheeks and jaws tightened. Fitch worked for Todd and that made him even madder. He wanted to dismantle his father's media empire. He wanted Todd to hurt.

Brandon watched the reporter slither away and his shoulders relaxed. Everyone else was just about gone, so he took a chance on trying to convince XJ that she should work with him instead of Fitch. He would take care of her. He would make sure that the world knew her story. He would do whatever it took to help her.

Brandon raked his hands through his hair and took a deep breath. He marched up to her. "I don't understand," he said, allowing the confusion to show. "Why would you agree to work with Fitch?"

So close to her, he realized how fragile she was. He wanted to pull her into an embrace but held back. He tried to focus on her response.

"I'm not going to win my mom's freedom by working with you," she said softly.

Brandon searched XJ's eyes. He could see the deep thought. Her shoulders dropped. "The Revolution can't help me. That's what got my family into this in the first place."

He did admire her straightforwardness. Brandon rubbed the back of his neck and tried to stay calm. It was hard. He kept his voice devoid of emotion. "Fitch will double cross you. He won't tell the truth about your family. He won't help you with your mom. He'll turn your story into something else. Revolution TV is...."

"I'm sick of the Revolution!" Brandon watched XJ perk up, flail her arms and put them on her hips. She took her finger and pointed it at his chest. "I don't want to hear about that stupid Revolution again. You sound like my mother and look where it's got her!"

Is she even listening to me? Brandon frowned. "You need to grab a clue XJ! CAGE plays for keeps. I wouldn't put it pass them to have Fitch on the payroll. You can't trust him."

XJ narrowed her eyes. "And am I suppose to trust you? The last time you didn't choose me. Last time you chose the establishment. Last time you chose Heather."

His voice cracked. "That was different! It wasn't what you thought!" Brandon wanted to explain what really happened that day a million times but he couldn't find the words. His public decision haunted him but he was trying to honor his mother.

"Who bankrolls Revolution TV?" XJ sneered. "Oh, that would be Daddy Miller right?"

Brandon shuddered. "I bankroll my own broadcast. My dad has nothing to do...."

XJ let out a disgusted sound. "Really? You're no better than Fitch! If your daddy told you not to run a story I'm pretty sure you'd do just what you're told. I'm pretty sure you'd forget about your revolutionary pipe dreams, and be the little rich brat that you are."

Brandon felt her ego blow in his gut. He did want to tell her story—he knew what was in his heart. He wanted to change the world and he'd use his dad's money, power, and fame.

But, he was still different from Fitch.

He stuffed his hands in his pockets. "Look, you're right," he said tonelessly. "You have no reason to trust me. What will I do different from Fitch? Well, I'll tell you: I'll respect your family. I'll respect you. Can you say that about Fitch?"

XJ moved closer and placed her hand on his shoulder. He kept his hands in his pockets, but wanted to take them out and touch her. He looked into her brown eyes and knew that this was much more than a story to him.

She said. "I respect your honesty. I know you believe in your heart that you'd do the right thing. I'm not sure if that's enough. CAGE wants to mind swipe my mom. I've got to go with a sure thing. Fitch is it."

The moment lingered. Both stood silent. His hands ached to touch her smooth chocolate skin. He wanted to hold her. Brandon closed his eyes and remembered the warmth of their embrace. He inched closer to her and the backyard washed away.

He wanted to show her tenderness and affection and he couldn't remember feeling this way about anyone. He certainly never felt this way about Heather. He wanted to tell her that he was a sure thing too.

"Fitch will double cross you." He let the words roll off his tongue.

"And, how do I know that I can put my trust in you?" XJ's voice shook.

He moved closer to her. He wanted to kiss her to make this all go away. "Don't trust me. Trust the Revolution. Your family has always gotten more from the Revolution than from the mainstream."

"My grandfather's dead," tears welled in her eyes. "My mother's on her way to having her mind swiped. And I'm seventeen trying to figure out what to do. I don't see what the Revolution has done so positive for my family."

He gently wiped away the falling tears from XJ's eyes. "Then don't put your trust in the Revolution. Put your trust in me."

"I trusted you once and it didn't work out well for me. I can't trust that you'll choose me over your designation type."

"Don't be foolish." *I want to kiss her so bad!*

"I'm not being foolish! I just want something out of this for me and my family this time!"

Brandon dropped his hand from her face. "Is that it? You want money?"

XJ stepped back from him. "Don't judge me. You choose money all the time. You chose her over me."

His neck tensed. *I wish I could explain what really happened!* "I'm not *with* her anymore! I don't use my dad's money for Revolution TV."

"Oh, forgive me! My mom just got hauled away! Now the little, reporter boy is offended, because I didn't know he broke up with his perfect girlfriend!"

"And you think handing your story over to that crook will help you?!" Brandon had had enough. He was ready to fight with her now.

"Get off my porch! Get off my land! Leave me alone!" XJ stormed away from him.

"I'll prove it to you!" he shouted at her back. "I'll prove that Fitch is no good! I'll prove you should stick with me!"

XJ was about to retort, when the trees moved. "Who's there?" She asked, looking frightened.

"Aghh! Aghh!" They heard a funny voice.

"Who is it?"

"XJ! XJ! I'm caught in the bushes! Help me—it's me Ziggy!"

Brandon let out a disgusted sound. *Not that class clown!*

XJ looked back over her shoulder, as she ran to help Ziggy. "Brandon, our conversation is over."

"I'll prove it to you." Brandon yelled back as he headed towards his car.

He'd find a way to convince her to see his side. But first, he'd have to stop thinking about how sexy she looked running toward the trees.

Chapter 9

"Brandon and you are the coolest, Heather. I hope when I find someone with the right mate-designation type that my relationship is as good as yours."

—Audience Member, GEP Network's Teen Sensation

Heather wanted to scream. She could have scratched XJ's eyes out. *How dare she get close to Brandon, again!* She already warned her once.

She balled up her fists and thought about what she'd like to do to XJ. Instead she stood up, slapped the dirt off her pants and watched Brandon walk back to his car.

Brandon is most important. She switched on her tracking ability and allowed it to fill her mind.

Her vision turned red. She knew her eyes had turned red too. Maybe she should punk XJ into leaving Brandon alone. Heather's nostrils flared as she saw her step sister running toward her, and over to another part of the burnt yard. Her breathing sped up.

Yeah, that's what I'll do! I'll show her! Heather's boots clunked across the gravel as she stepped out of hiding and walked up behind XJ.

"I need to talk to you." Heather saw the back of XJ's hair through red eyes. She put her hands on her hips.

"I'm sorry." Her step sister said, without even turning around. "You've missed the bulletin. Fitch already has my exclusive."

Irritation burned Heather and her stomach boiled. "I'm not here to write a story about you! I'm here to—!"

Someone leaped out of the bushes and hugged XJ tight. "Please—!" Heather said with annoyance. She'd recognized him from school. *What's his name? Ziggy. That's it! She hangs out with losers!*

She tapped her foot. "Don't you hear me talking to you?" Ziggy smiled at her and before she realized it, he'd pounced on her.

Heather stumbled back, as she peeled him off. "Don't touch me, freak!" But Ziggy touched her everywhere. He made his way to releasing her perfect ponytail. Heather's blond hair fell down to her shoulders. Ziggy raced away with her hair clip. Her lips parted and her eyes widened.

"Give that back to me! You little turd!" Heather tried to catch him but he moved *quick.*

He talked so fast and moved at lightening speeds. Her eyes couldn't keep up with his movements. Her hands shook.

Not now! She had to focus. She needed another white pill bad.

Heather closed her eyes and tapped deeper into her tracking ability: the part of her that was both tracker and hunter. Heather tracked Ziggy's mind trail as if she could smell his scent. She held up her arm like a speed breaker catching Ziggy in his chest. Ziggy bounced backwards and fell hitting the back of his puffy Afro on the ground.

He screamed a decade a minute."I diddn't mmmean itt! I just wannniitt toooo sssseee itttt!"

Heather ignored him. She jumped on top of his chest and held his arm down with her knee. His body squirmed as he screamed. "DDDon't hurt me whiteee gUrrl! GGett Off! III justtt wwwannna seeee ittt!"

Heather put her face down to his. *"Mine* you turd! Mine! Keep your grubby hands off!" She wrenched her hair clip from his hand. Her body started to shake.

Not now! Not now. She thought. *I've got to keep control.*

But the other Heather swarmed inside her mind. *Really?* the voice said. *You're really beatin' up on this helpless child? Let me out!*

Heather grabbed her head. *No. No. You can't come out! I'm busy.*

Heather snapped back and saw someone heading towards her. She rolled off the little butterscotch-colored Ziggy.

"You're hurting him!" It was XJ.

"He should've kept his hands off me!" Heather yelled.

"He's got a disorder. He can't help it. He's got advanced GEP ADD. It causes him to move fast and fixate on small items." XJ helped Ziggy off the ground and began picking dirt out of his Afro.

"You two are freaking idiots!" Heather whined.

XJ stopped patting Ziggy and took a closer look at her. "Heather? *WTF?* What do you want uppity, white girl? Here to gloat for your mother? I really don't have time for you or your mama!" She finished cleaning Ziggy off, and turned her back on her step sister.

Heather started to shake. Her other voice railed inside her mind. *Let's go. Let me out. You don't need to do this. The girl already has enough to deal with.*

She felt her mind melting down. *"Shut up!"* She said inside and outside her head; and shook off the other personality. Her vision turned red again, and she dug deep into her hunter self.

She wanted to spit on XJ. "I'm not here for my mother. I'm here to tell you to keep your hands off my man."

XJ took a deep breath and turned around. Her fists were clenched. "Really? Are you really here about Brandon? CAGE takes my mom away and all you can think about is your little rich, boy toy?"

"If I can remember correctly, this isn't the first time you tried to steal my man!" Heather spat, pointing her finger. "Didn't you learn your lesson the first time?"

"Brandon chose you just like my father chose your stupid mother!" XJ shot back. "Isn't that enough for you? Leave me alone!" She turned her back to her step sister again and led little Ziggy towards her house.

I'm going to claw her eyes out! The hunter popped into her mind and Heather charged towards XJ. She almost had her hands around XJ's braids, when the girl whipped around to face her.

XJ's eyes had turned gray. That's when Heather realized that she couldn't move. She wanted to scream but nothing came out. Just then her step sister's face came into view.

Her words were muffled. "I don't want Brandon. I'm more worried about my mom. Now get off my land before I forget you're my step sister and hurt you, white girl."

Heather felt something flash inside the front of her eyes. The door to XJ's house closed.

"You tramp!" Heather screamed.

She blacked out.

She came too, breathing deeply. "Ah, finally out...." Her second personality had taken over. "I need to get outta here!"

The other Heather railed inside her mind. *Let me out!* She raged and screamed. But the Heather now in control knew better than to release her.

Not now anyway. The new Heather walked back to her car—all the while feeling sorry for her step sister and what was going to happen. *Maybe I have time to stop it.*

She slid into her car. Her shoulders slumped and she cried on the steering wheel.

But the thick emotion allowed the first Heather to slip back in control. This one hated XJ. Heather bent the rear view mirror to her face, and fixed her make-up. She laughed hysterically. "You won't be able to save that little jungle bunny!"

Trapped inside herself. The other Heather felt bad. Their plan was in motion. She knew she couldn't stop it. *XJ is in trouble and it's all my fault.*

"Stop feeling sorry for her! She tried to steal my man!" The outside Heather mashed the gas and skidded away. "Serves the slut right!"

Chapter 10

This generation of GEPs has a rendezvous with destiny.
—Dr. Gary Leonard Kates, Press Conference

XJ hopped up onto the porch landing, opened the front door, waited for Ziggy to enter and slammed the door. She turned to face the ransacked living room—the couch and chairs overturned in the aftermath of a serious battle.

She felt sick. This was the worst day of her life. Her back crashed against the closed door, as she slid into a declining slump all the way to the floor. Uncontrollable air gasps escaped her throat as her head fell between her knees.

Her life was falling apart and she felt powerless to do anything about it. Tears and moans soaked the inside of her jacket. She could barely hear Ziggy consoling her. What was she going to do? How would she save her mother? Could she trust Fitch?

XJ slowly pulled herself together. She felt Ziggy rub her back and shoulders. He was the best friend she'd ever had even though he had an ADD problem.

Ziggy said in his rapid speech "Iiii'mmmm ss-sso soooroorrry, mmmaaannnn. Justttt sooo sorrrrry."

XJ wiped her face. "It's not your fault. I'll figure this out."

They both sat in silence, while her mind raced through the afternoon's events. She remembered the last conversation with Dorothy, about a stupid ring and meeting Brockman. XJ searched the jacket pockets and stood up. Her fingers emerged with a glowing, platinum ruby ring.

"WWWoooeeee, whhhhhatt's thatt ttthing?" Ziggy sputtered, while his eyes twinkled like he'd been struck with a fixation bug.

"Something my mom gave me." She slid the ring on her finger.

The ring pinched her *hard*. Blood trickled down her finger. "Ouch!" XJ yelled. *"WTF?!"* She shook her hand, and tried to pull the ring off but it refused to budge.

"LLLLet mmme! LLLLLet me hhhavee itt!" Ziggy grabbed her hand and tried to wrench it off.

A female computerized voice spoke from the ring. *"Genetic match. Code grandchild activated."*

"Ouch! Stop Ziggy! Now's not the time." XJ jerked her hand away and nursed it.

While Ziggy bounced up and down, his Afro bounced like a little tiger. "SSSSomethhhhing's gllllowwwwinggg."

The ring was glowing ... with blue light.

XJ blinked as dots raced in front of her eyes. She staggered and her head felt woozy. A voice told her not to let him touch anything. But her mind felt submerged in deep water. She couldn't hold her balance.

Her head swam. She couldn't stop him. "Ziggy—*no!*" Her mind tried to hold on, while the flood of information plunged her deeper. It was too late.

"Oooo. CCCaaann III kkEEEpp...." Ziggy jerked, grabbing a silver lamp, as electric, blue light shocked his body.

XJ sank to her knees trying to handle the cranium splitting headache ... Ziggy's screams sounded faint ... she grabbed her head.

"Ziggy?" She asked disorientated. A high, pitched sound pierced her mind. Covering her ears, she crumpled in a deafening scream. Everything stopped.... There was nothingness.... Her mind sucked back like a computer reboot.

She didn't remember how it happened but she was on the floor, and her face hurt. She rolled over.

A faint, male voice now hummed inside her head. *"You can help your friend if you replace the chipset lamps back in their places. You have to place them over the optical motherboards in the floor."*

She rose and weakly used her telekinetic ability to place the furniture back. Finally, her mother's three silver lamps were the only items left to be replaced. XJ looked over at Ziggy. His Afro smelled like it been scorched by a nasty hot comb. She hoped that he'd be okay.

She walked over to the location where she knew the lamp belonged and examined the floor. A blue, optical motherboard lived in the floor socket. Using her ability, she lifted the first lamp out of Ziggy's open hand and placed it over the socket. It clicked in place. One by one she replaced the other lamps. Once the last lamp connected, a darker blue light in the shape of a triangle connected the room.

The female voice intoned, *"Program complete."*

A door swung open next to the kitchen, and a holographic man's face popped out. XJ squinted and shook her head. Was she seeing things? That's when she realized that it was someone she recognized.

"Granddad? Granddad Kates? Is that *you?"*

The same male voice spoke. "Yes, doll. It's me. Well, what's left of me, anyway. Bring your friend inside my lab and we'll see if we can't revive him."

XJ took a step towards Ziggy and the doorbell rang. She looked at her grandfather and the wall opening.

She raked her hands through her hair and frowned. "What am I supposed to do?"

XJ watched the ring loosen from her finger, and roll underneath the couch. She let out an irritated sigh. The doorbell rang again.

"I'll close the door. They won't know I'm here. Don't worry doll. I'll let you in." XJ watched her grandfather disappear and the lab door slam shut.

She grumbled and stomped to the front door. "The story of my freaking life. Can't anything ever be normal?"

Ziggy moaned and she glanced at him. She'd have to get rid of whoever this was, so her grandfather could help him.

Chapter 11

"The nearer GEPs come to the truth, the more dangerous their mission becomes."

—John Brockman, News Conference

Brandon closed the door of his Mustang and walked down the Decatur, Georgia block to the *GEP Daily Post,* his father's online newspaper. He loved downtown Decatur. The storefront businesses were rad and different. He liked the look.

He balled up his right fist and ground it into his open left hand. He had to figure out a way to convince XJ that Fitch was a fraud.

Brandon pushed the door open and marched into the building. His black combat boots echoed and the long belt chain that held his keys jingled. He ran his hand through his blond hair to make sure it spiked enough. Dressed in black jeans and an oversized black sweatshirt, he felt ready for espionage.

He walked to the elevator and got on. He'd been here with his dad before but this time it was different. No one was around since it was so late in the day. If he was lucky, Fitch wouldn't be here either.

Brandon got off on the third floor and walked into the reception area. He had to play this smooth, if he wanted to get into Fitch's office.

He looked at the receptionist. She was young and anorexic looking, with dark hair and really pale skin. She'd be easy enough to fool. He gave her his best smile to distract her while he lightly touched the top of her computer.

"Hey sweetness." Brandon moved himself closer so he could use his technopathic ability to add himself onto Fitch's calendar.

The wiry girl smiled. "Oh, may I help you?" She lifted a pencil to her mouth and tapped the eraser on her lips.

Brandon sensed his technopathic ability warm. Inside his mind's eye, he could view her computer monitor. His hacking ability moved quick so it only took a few seconds to add his name to the calendar.

"I have an appointment with Mr. Fitch. He's working on a story with me." Brandon said glibly.

"Um ... Mr. Fitch is currently in an important meeting. I'm sure he's booked for the evening. Are you sure your appointment is for today?" The receptionist used the pencil to punch at her keyboard. "What was your name?" She smiled and looked up.

"Jay ... Jay Arthur. We're supposed to meet today." Brandon straightened up and stepped back from the desk.

"I don't know how I missed this. Come on back, Jay ... um, Mr. Arthur." The receptionist opened the door and escorted Brandon to Fitch's office.

Brandon cautiously scanned the newsroom. The place was pretty empty. There were only a few reporters who didn't seem the least bit interested in anything, except what was going on inside their own worlds.

Brandon relaxed and followed the receptionist. "Would you like coffee, tea or soda?" she asked.

"Um. Nope." Brandon stuffed his hands deep inside his pockets and kept walking. He just wanted to get in to see what Fitch was hiding.

"Here we are." The receptionist smiled. She would've been cute if she wasn't so skinny.

Brandon smiled back at her and walked into Fitch's office. Cigarette smoke made him hold his breath for a minute. *Fitch must be a chain smoker.... The office is a nice size, though.*

"Thanks ... I'll sit over here." Brandon swiped his nose and pointed at a chair across the room.

"Mr. Fitch should be with you momentarily." The receptionist smiled her way out of the room with hopeful eyes. The door clicked and Brandon headed towards Fitch's desk. He saw what he needed amongst the OCD organized desk: Fitch's Tablet PC.

Brandon plopped down in the reporter's chair and put his boots on the desk. He needed to relax for this. He tapped into his ability and mentally dropped down into the tablet PC. Brandon smiled inside as he broke the encryption sequence. His mind melded with the PC and absorbed what was on it quickly.

His ability hummed throughout his mind and body. It felt good. His mind hacked deeper. He knew there was something hidden behind this weird firewall.

He'd *found* it! The proof he needed to show XJ!

He was about to store the information inside the recesses of his mind when the biomechanical virus took him down fast. He slapped himself mentally. He'd been careless. He pulled back inside his mind. The virus attacked and tried to rewrite his central nervous system. Brandon screamed inside his mind.

"Ugh!" He dropped the tablet on the floor to sever the connection but it was too late.

The biomechanical virus infected him. He fought the virus internally. His whole body collapsed on the floor and he went into convulsions. A succession of *1-00-11-00-0-1-01* flashed across his eyes.

Shaking, he stared at the ceiling. He thought about XJ ... her cute brown eyes, soft pecan colored skin, and sexy shape. He'd wanted to prove that Fitch was bad. That she should choose him. Mate-designation type or not.

Who would help her now?

Brandon moaned. He lifted a shaky hand to his forehead and swiped the sweat from his brow. This was all Fitch's fault! Fitch worked for Todd Miller! *His father!*

Brandon pounded the round of his fists on the floor. He wanted to discredit his dad. He wanted to show the world that the man was a fraud and couldn't be trusted.

Brandon rolled his head back and forth. He went in and out of delusion ... drifting towards his mother. He missed her....

In a surreal moment, his mind jumped into a memory. Her beautiful eyes, loving touch, soothing voice relaxed his body. Warmth spread throughout him. A small swell of anger lingered. His mother had the ability to heal everyone except herself.

He could feel her power blossom within him. Where the virus was hot and fast, the healing was slow, cool. His body stopped, rebalanced and rebooted, but full healing would take time.

Voices snapped him back to reality. He needed to hide! He rolled over. His head still swam and pounded. Voices moved closer. He dragged himself into a small dark corner and scrunched up his legs.

It wasn't the best hiding spot. He was tall and it was hard for him to compress his body, but he did. Hopefully, no one would notice him and he could get away.

He recognized Fitch's voice and someone familiar. He looked at his skin. The number code *1-00-11-00-0-1-01* still slithered along his skin. The voices entered the room. Brandon tried to push back further into his hiding space.

"Yes, yes, Mr. Miller. I was able to secure the interview with the Patterson girl." Fitch was irritating, but Todd's presence made Brandon's stomach turn.

"Just make sure you don't fly off the cuff, Fitch. I don't want this slapping the Network in the face."

He's playing a game! I knew it! He wanted to lash out, but his head swam. *Later ... I'll get him later.* Now, he needed to heal.

"I'll do my best, sir. There won't be a repeat of that last incident." Fitch whined.

"Look, the mother was a revolutionary nut," Todd went on. "And this daughter doesn't look like she's wrapped too tight. I don't know what she'll say. But to cover all of our butts, it's better if you let me see the article before it's run. I don't want any surprises."

His dad's words slapped Brandon out of illness. *How dare he talk about XJ like that?*

He moaned loudly, and sprung out of the corner—physically lashing out at the blotched figure that closely resembled his father's shape. But his body was too weak.

His father side-stepped the attack easily. *"Brandon? What are you doing here?"*

The words were clear in Brandon's head, but came out in muddled confusion. "You caann't st ... op th ... e trute!"

He tried to tongue lash Todd, but the room continued to spiral and spin out of control. The viral code skittered and skimmed faster across his body.

He lost consciousness in his dad's arms staring into Fitch's hostile grin.

Brandon awoke believing that he was still dreaming about his mother.

"Mom?" He called out.

"Shh...." He heard a calming voice. Someone fluffed his pillow and wiped the sweat from his brow.

"It's okay, Brandon. You're safe now."

He rolled over in his bed. Something was bothering him. But he couldn't remember what it was. He just wanted to rest.

How did I get in bed?

He pushed the covers back and leapt up, as he remembered his dad's conversation with Fitch and the story.

The servants scrambled to his bedside and he was hit with questions. *"Are you alright?"*

"Does it still hurt?"

"How do you feel?"

Yadda, yadda ... just leave me alone. Disturbed and agitated he yelled, "Where's my father?"

Everything went still. His android, Nicki, said in a calm, mechanized voice, *"Mr. Miller has been delayed at a business meeting. He will return shortly."*

"Get *out!* Get out all off you!" Brandon screamed, throwing pillows everywhere. Tears pushed behind his eyes, but he refused to allow them to flow.

His father had made a choice to hide the truth. And now, Brandon had made his.

He hobbled to the dresser and found his cell phone. He'd send a text to XJ, but how would he explain all of this to her? He still didn't quite have the proof he needed to convince her to choose him and not Fitch.

Chapter 12

"We have information to suggest that CAGE abducts the strongest of us and takes us to a special lab called Zone 6. Many have lost their minds in that place."

—Dorothy Kates-Patterson, Revolutionary News Conference

XJ stomped to the front door. She released an angry breath. Things were always falling apart or something crazy happening. How weird was it for her to have a holographic grandfather? Then, there was all of the craziness that led to Ziggy getting electrocuted.

Ziggy moaned softly, and she frowned. *Is this another reporter? I can't take one more thing!*

XJ shook off her angst, and opened the door to face a pudgy-faced, brown-skinned woman with a short, relaxed hairstyle. She was dressed in a bland, brown suit and low-heeled shoes.

"Can I help you?" *Can this day get any worse?*

"Are you the offspring of Dorothy Kates-Patterson?" the tall woman asked.

XJ folded her arms across her chest. "Who wants to know?"

The woman didn't make any eye contact with her. She held up a long sensor that blasted a red scan across XJ's eyes. "Confirmed."

"Who are you? Are you another reporter?" XJ squinted, trying to adjust her eyes after the blinding light.

"My name is Anne Hughes. I'm a social worker. Usually, I wouldn't work a case such as yours. But Joanne Chesimard appears to be ... umm, busy so you have me. Pack your bags."

XJ kept her arms folded and tensed her shoulders. "What? I'm not going anywhere with you!"

Anne Hughes moved closer so that they were face to face. "Oh, yes, you are. You're a 17-year old minor. One parent is in custody and the other is out of the country. You're on your way to foster care."

XJ's heart beat faster. She tried to control the panic rolling through her system. "No, you don't understand. I'm very independent and quite capable of—"

Ms. Hughes sucked in her tongue against her front gold tooth and made a disgusted sound. "Humph. A reasoner. You won't be able to reason out of this. You aren't safe on the streets alone. Minor GEPs are incapable of following the proper laws without parental units. Pack your things."

XJ took a step back. "Do you know what I've been through today? Can't you pick me up tomorrow? Surely, I can stay one night alone."

Ziggy made a moaning sound in the background. Ms. Hughes pushed XJ out of the way to see Ziggy. She sneered."Obviously minor GEPs can't be left unattended."

XJ tried to talk but her head began to tingle. She faintly heard Ms. Hughes' voice while a hazy wall slowly spread across her mind. She lost her ability to think. She couldn't control herself. She was a puppet. XJ saw Ms. Hughes' mouth moving ... her mind was being twisted back and forth until she did exactly what Anne Hughes wanted. She tried to snap back, but the sensation couldn't be stopped.

Ms. Hughes said, "Don't fight it. Let it happen. You'll be safer in Zone 6."

XJ shuddered. People who went to Zone 6 never returned. Would she ever see her mother again? She tried to fight back. The mind film stuck even closer. The more she fought the more entrapped she became. Her mind felt like gluey sand—sticky and dirty.

XJ moved stiffly and mechanically. She went to her room and packed an overnight bag while time slipped away. Everything seemed like a mind-induced horror. Helpless, she walked into the living room and saw a CAGE officer picking up Ziggy.

Deep inside, she yelled a blood-curdling scream while outside her body moved according to Ms. Hughes' instructions. A part of XJ watched in terror as her body performed tasks without her consent like she was Anne Hughes' finger-puppet.

She grabbed her jacket with her audio gun and overnight bag. She glided down the porch stairs and slid into the government vehicle. Fighting back was useless, but she still tried. Fury and rage fumed inside until her body slumped, blacked out and shut down.

XJ's eyes popped open when her head bumped. Groggy and confused she tried to reconnect the dots as she scanned the back seat of the SUV. She rubbed her temples. She had a monster headache. The inside of the car was dark, and she allowed her head to gently bump to the left to see if Ziggy was okay.

Ziggy made slow moaning noises. XJ moved her hand on top of his and squeezed. She lowered her head and swallowed, then squeezed her eyes shut.

It's my fault that Ziggy is in this situation, she thought. How would she get them out of this? *I need a plan. I need to fix this so that both of us are safe.*

Shaking off her anxiety, she popped her eyes open and used her telekinetic ability to unlatch the lock on the door. It was hard for her to see out of the dark windows and into the passing trees along Highway-78.

But she knew they'd have a secure hiding place if they were able to roll out on the busy highway and hide in the underbrush. She craned her neck up to look out the window. It looked like they were getting close to the Stone Mountain CAGE facility gate.

XJ sensed that the social worker might be watching them in the mirror so she quickly smashed her eyelids together. She saw a rainbow of dots and splashes flutter across her eyelids.

She used this quiet moment to focus on waking Ziggy. She opened one eye and gently nudged him with her telekinetic ability. Ziggy toppled over.

Shaking with fear, he almost announced that they were both awake. XJ tried to soothe him. She made deliberate, hand gestures towards the door so that he'd pick up on her escape idea.

Ziggy's floppy Afro shook, as horror spread across his face like a yellow streak. XJ couldn't calm him down. She knew that his ADD GEP condition could become erratic at times—even uncontrollable—but this was *intense*.

She placed her finger to her lips and tried to calm him. Anxious tears strolled down his butterscotch colored face. He gave a terror-filled scream, as Ms. Hughes crushed the brakes to a screeching halt and turned around.

"I knew you two were awake." XJ saw Ms. Hughes' mouth move in slow motion. She turned her head and heard a mad frenzy on Highway-78. Tires screeched, squealed and screamed. She realized this might be her only chance to get away.

She felt the social worker's ability lulling her back into a deep trance. But she resisted. She felt a wall begin to erect within her mind. XJ pulled out her audio gun.

"Ziggy!" XJ yelled. "We've got to get out of here!"

Ziggy appeared to be buried between terror and deep trance. He didn't speak. He shook his head back and forth, until it looked like it would explode. XJ lifted her audio gun to shoot the social worker but the shot went wild.

"Damn!" She yelled.

With all the commotion she couldn't get off another shot and the gun fell from her hands. She used her telekinetic ability to push the door open, and pull Ziggy forward. But he ground in his heels and fell back into the SUV, as XJ spilled out onto Highway-78 ... into oncoming traffic.

Her life flashed before her eyes in a barrage of headlights and more tire screeches. Her heart sucked inside her soul, as she hopped over stopped cars and bolted for the tree line.

Ziggy must have caused a distraction. The SUV appeared to give up the chase. XJ watched the black SUV speed off towards the facility entrance.

It was hard to catch her breath. What would she do now? How would she get out of the trees and back home? Worse yet, how would she save Ziggy?

She found a quiet place to sit and think. *My life is so far from normal it's pitiful. I always have these impossible situations to deal with. And now I'm crying again!*

Wiping her eyes, she felt her pocket buzzing. Brandon had sent her a text. She texted him back. She took a deep breath and her body went limp. At least she'd have a way home until she could figure out her next step.

Chapter 13

Of all the discoveries that GEPs need to make, the most important is to learn to trust one another, implicitly.
—John Brockman

Brandon skidded his Mustang onto the median. His tires crackled over the debris and stopped. He jumped out of the car and squinted. The spring air was cool and it was beginning to get dark. He left the car running with the high beam lights on.

His stomach clenched when he saw the heavy, oncoming traffic. But he couldn't spot XJ.

How did she end up out here? He sprinted to the tree in the underbrush. "XJ!" He called out. "XJ where are you?"

Brandon pushed through the fallen trees and weeds. A flash of light caught his attention. He turned around and refocused his eyes. It was a black SUV. The vehicle was further down the road but he knew it held CAGE officers. His heart beat faster. He had to find her _quick_.

_"XJ!"_ He allowed his panic to be heard.

"Here, I am..." a voice called faintly. He spotted her in a nearby bush, and looked into her eyes. "We've got to get out of here." He raced over to her and grabbed her arm to help her move faster.

"I'm okay ... I can walk." She sounded like she'd been crying, and his heart went out to her.

"Hey ... are you sure you're alright?" Brandon asked, wiping a tear from her soft cheek. He wanted to take her into his arms right there. But he saw the headlights from the CAGE vehicle moving closer to his Mustang.

"We need to hurry. That looks like CAGE officers." The two of them took off towards his car.

"Halt." A male, computerized voice ordered over a loud speaker. *"Your vehicle must submit to a CAGE search."* .

"C'mon! I can lose them!" He raced to the passenger side door and opened it for her. The CAGE vehicle moved up. It would be on top of them in a minute! Brandon slid across the hood of his Mustang to the other side and hopped into the driver's seat.

"It's time to *roll!"* He touched the console and the Mustang roared to life.

Two CAGE officers were barreling towards his Mustang, when he sped from zero to sixty onto the highway. Horns blared, but he didn't care. He closed his eyes and tapped into the computer controls.

He opened his eyes and turned towards XJ. She seemed a little shaken, but her eyes looked thoughtful.

"No worries. I got this." He smiled and mashed the gas.

"That's what I'm afraid of...." XJ smiled at her own joke. "I might've been safer with those CAGE officers." To Brandon she looked tired ... but beautiful.

He allowed his Mustang to pick up a little more speed. He wanted distance between them and the enemy. Hopefully, there wouldn't be any more pursuits. That's when he saw flashing lights coming up from behind.

"Crap! There's more of them!" He tapped the console of his Mustang's computer again. This time he allowed his ability to go deeper. He needed maps and a plan to lose CAGE.

"Brandon, watch out!" XJ screamed as he used his ability to bypass cars blocking them.

He drove in the bike lane and on the sidewalk to get away. His adrenaline was pumping, but no way was he going to allow CAGE to catch them.

"OMG!" XJ sounded like she was blowing a gasket.

"Just close your eyes. We're fine ... I have a plan." Brandon found what he needed. He made a sharp turn on Highway-124 and into more traffic. CAGE was close, yet still far enough away that his plan would work.

He glanced at XJ again. She was mouthing a prayer. Brandon reached over and squeezed her hand—racing down 124, ducking, dodging and rolling at lightning speed.

Finally, they made it to the mall. "We'll ditch them here." He looked over at her and smiled. She didn't look amused.

He whipped into the parking deck and turned off his car. "Made it!" He winked at her.

"WTF! Brandon you almost killed us!" XJ shouted hysterically. "I can't believe you drive like that! Have you lost your *mind?*"

"C'mon.... We better go." Brandon hopped out, opened his trunk and pulled his car cover out, while XJ slid out. He put the cover over his ride and put his Letterman's jacket over her shoulders.

"In order for my plan to work, we need to pretend that we're a couple. Can you handle that?" He pulled the jacket up over her and pulled a few twigs from her hair.

XJ looked up at him with venom. "I could kill you!"

"I know, but can you be my girlfriend?" He kissed her on the forehead and she made a disgusted huffing noise.

Setting the alarm on his car, they walked through the crowded, parking deck. He heard sirens but the CAGE vehicles were on a lower level.

They walked through the doors and were instantly hit with fluorescent lights. He pulled XJ closer into a lover's embrace, and she stiffened up. "Don't look so uncomfortable. Act natural ... like we've been together for a while."

"You aggravate me!"

"Are you hungry?" He put his arm around her waist and kissed her cheek.

XJ gritted her teeth. "I want to claw your eyes out!"

They rounded the corner, saw five mall cops and CAGE officers headed towards them. Brandon stopped and pulled XJ into a corner area.

"Shh ... don't freak." He look deep into her eyes and touched his mouth to hers.

He knew the kiss wasn't real but he couldn't help it. The soft touch of her lips ignited something in him. He wanted more ... so he opened his mouth and kissed her for real. He thought XJ wouldn't kiss him back, but she reciprocated hot and heavy.

Her arms encircled his neck. His manhood rose and he pulled her closer into his embrace. She broke the kiss and stared deeply into his eyes.

Then, XJ broke her gaze and looked around. "They're gone ... and everybody's staring at us."

The other mall customers turned their heads away. One of them, an elderly woman retorted, "You two should be ashamed!"

Brandon smiled and grabbed her hand. *God, I want her bad!* "Come on ... let's get something to eat." They walked over to a *Chilly's* and asked for a booth.

XJ looked sheepish. "I don't have any money."

"I got this." Brandon puffed out his chest. *It's the least I can do. She looks tired and hungry ... but she's still gorgeous.*

The waitress seated them. He studied her face as she read the menu. *I like seeing her in my jacket.* He thought about what happened the previous summer. *I wish I could take it all back. I made a bad choice. I really wanted XJ, but I picked Heather.*

But not this time. He'd made his choice. Now he just needed to figure out how to get her to choose him. They made small talk until the food came. He watched her eat her burger. And then he realized she still needed help.

Brandon leaned closer. "What are you going to do about Fitch and your story?"

"Do you ever stop?" She let out an exasperated sigh and sat back. "I just want to free my mom! I think Fitch can help me."

"You can't trust him." He smashed his fist on the table, realized he was coming on a little strong and calmed down. "Look, I don't exactly have proof, but I visited his office. I sort of hacked into his computer and got a bad biomechanical virus."

"You hacked into the man's *computer?*" XJ looked horrified.

Brandon squared his shoulders and sat erect. "Well ... how else would I find the stuff that he's doing that's not right?"

XJ shook her head in disgust, shifting her body away from him. "If you hacked my computer, I'd give you a virus, too! That doesn't prove anything!"

"He's hiding something." His voice cracked a little. "Revolutionaries need to get to the truth, otherwise we'll be looking like fools." Brandon could see the anger mounting but he had to get through to her.

She drummed her fingers on the edge of the table. "I'm so sick of this revolutionary bull! You sound just like my mom! You're no better than CAGE!"

An awkward silence passed between them. Suddenly, they were surrounded by the *Chilly's* crew. "Happy Birthday!" They sung a funny tune. The young couple couldn't help but laugh.

Finally, one of the waiters asked, "Who's the birthday person?"

Brandon and XJ said together, "Neither."

The waiter looked embarrassed. "We're so sorry!" One of the other waiters pointed to a guy signaling them to come over.

"It's okay." Brandon gave an easy laugh. "Just add it to our bill. You made my girlfriend smile." He winked at XJ.

The waiter ran into the back to get another cake and, within minutes, they heard the birthday song again. Eating the cake, they relaxed a little.

I enjoy spending time with XJ, he thought; smiling at her. *She really holds her ground and I can appreciate that.* Out the corner of his eye, he saw the mall cops and CAGE officers heading their way.

"Let's get out of here!" Pulling out more than enough cash to cover the bill and tip, he escorted XJ out the side door. The fire alarm went off and they ignored it. They needed the distraction.

They walked quickly back to his Mustang, and he whipped the cover off, stashing it back in the trunk and smoothing his hand over his ride. He used his ability to tap into the car's computer and change the paint color to black; along with the license plate. Now they were riding in REVOLUTION 1 instead of GEPFREE. He hustled her into the car and they took off.

On the way out of the deck, they passed the CAGE officers and mall cops. Brandon smiled. CAGE wouldn't get them today.

Chapter 14

"You'll never get anywhere playing CAGE's game the way CAGE says. Sometimes you've got to take matters into your own hands to find out the truth. "

—Dorothy Kates-Patterson, News Conference

The ride to her house went smooth and easy. He couldn't believe how much he'd enjoyed dinner with her. Underneath it all, he knew that they had differences, but he liked the fact that she tested his ideas.

He pulled around to the back road entrance to her home. If they went in the front door, they were both afraid that CAGE might see them and take her away. Brandon followed XJ through red clay, downed trees, and brush.

He thought about his own home. It was perfectly manicured with the mansion as the center piece. Not one tree or bush stood in the way of the view. It stood out like a true plantation mansion. He realized that the two of them were from two different worlds. But they could still share laughter and tragedy.

Brandon tried to focus on making it to her home, and how he could convince her to give him the exclusive for Revolution TV. But his mind kept wandering to her coca-cola bottle shape. He wanted to reach out and touch her. Before he knew it, he'd slammed into her rear-end.

"Ouch!" XJ toppled over. "Can you watch it?"

"I'm sorry." He mumbled. "My mind was somewhere else...."

They continued until they reached the path to her house. XJ visually scouted the area. "Everything looks clear."

She moved toward her house, but Brandon held her back. He used the power line to tap into her home's computerized network. Using his ability, he searched for any electronic booby traps. He mentally bumped into a trip wire on the front door, but the windows were clear.

He also stumbled into a firewall. It seemed odd because he sensed it wasn't set-up by CAGE.

XJ pursed her lips. "Did you use your hacking ability?"

"I had to make sure you were safe. You can't go through the front door but the windows are fine." He rubbed his forehead. He forgot that he was still recovering from that virus.

"Next time, ask before you hack into my home." XJ sashayed to the back window.

"You're welcome, sweetheart." Brandon fired back sarcastically, following the flow of her hips with his eyes.

XJ let out a short, "Humph!"

It was dark, but she found a window that was unlatched, pushed it up and slid into her kitchen. Brandon followed. As he entered, the two collided. Her backside slide across his groin and he had to catch himself.

"Excuse me," he whispered. "I didn't mean to be so close." He blew a little breath on the back of her neck and she elbowed him in the stomach.

Her brown eyes glistened in the moonlight. *She's so beautiful....* The urge to pull her close and kiss her overwhelmed him. *If I try to kiss her again, she might take it the wrong way. But that kiss at the mall was good....*

"You don't have to stay. I'll be safe."

"I'll stay, just in case you want to talk some more—I mean, about Fitch or your story. I'd be willing to listen." He moved nearer to her. *God, her lips are cute, brown, and kissable.*

XJ turned her head. "Um, let me see if we have anything in the frig. Would you like a drink or something?"

Brandon peered into the refrigerator. "Is this all you have?" He was used to having several pantries full of snacks.

"I'm sorry, rich boy. We only have the bare essentials. You can have bottled water or bottled water. Which one do you want?"

He realized that he'd offended her. "I didn't mean it like that. I just meant...."

"Save it!" XJ snapped. "Look you can leave anytime you get ready. I'm used to making it by myself." She slammed the refrigerator and folded her arms.

Brandon knew that he'd shown himself to be a snob. Embarrassed he gazed deeply into her eyes. "I ... I didn't mean anything by it. I'm really thirsty. I'd love to have some bottled water."

XJ shrugged, opened the refrigerator back up and tossed the bottle of water at him as she moved into the living room.

Pulling out her cell phone, and using her finger to check her messages, she said. "Look, you don't have to stay, I'll be fine."

Even in the low light of the moon, he could tell that the living room was a mess. "I guess you can't turn on any lights or that might signal CAGE. I can stop by after school tomorrow and try to help you straighten up."

"That won't be necessary." XJ crossed her legs and flopped down on the couch.

Her voice squeaked ... she began to softly cry. He didn't know how to react. Inside he wanted to hold her and make it better. He wanted to take away her pain. She seemed so fragile. She reminded him of his mother, strong but delicate.

Trying not to make any sudden moves, he eased his way next to her and positioned himself so that her head could rest on his shoulder. He had a strong urge to kiss her again, but he held back and stroked her braids while she cried. He understood her feelings on some level.

The moonlight streaked her pecan-colored face and his body began to react to her. It seemed natural. And yet he'd never felt like this about a girl before. In fact the only girl that he'd gone all the way with was Heather and it didn't feel like this.

Something about XJ was special. He rubbed his chin across her forehead and took in a deep breath. He enjoyed the way she smelled and wanted to....

"Thanks Brandon. I appreciate the fact that you're here. Since Ziggy's gone I don't have any friends to support me."

Friends! He certainly did not want to be her friend. *Ugh!* "You're welcome. You know, I could support you more if you let me get the exclusive on your story."

XJ recoiled. Cold air shot between them. "Is that what this is? You want to get the exclusive."

"No, of course not! But it would be nice if...." Brandon tried to get her to calm down but she moved further from his touch.

"Oh, I know." XJ leaped off of the couch and moved as far away from him as possible. "Just get out!"

"I didn't mean it like that...," Brandon stammered. "I mean...." A lost memory popped into his head from his experience with Fitch's computer. He rubbed the temples on both sides of his forehead.

"I know that Fitch is bad. I can't prove it but look at me. Why would a reporter need to have a biomechanical virus on his computer? What's he hiding?"

He could see her angry face in the low light. "Oh, I should believe the word of a computer hacker? Get out!"

Brandon didn't want to go. He knew there was something special between them. "I'm sorry. I didn't mean to upset you." He held his shoulders low and scooted off the couch.

XJ walked him to the kitchen window—all the while ranting. "Get out and don't come back! Of all the nerve! Coming in here and pretending to be my friend; when all you really wanted was the story!"

Brandon tried to explain, but couldn't get the words out. He slunk down and climbed out of the window. XJ slammed it shut and locked it. He couldn't make her understand. He did want the exclusive. But what he really wanted was to hang out with XJ.

How can I prove to her that I'm on the up-and-up?

Chapter 15

"A GEP Revolutionary always pops up close to CAGE."
—Anonymous Revolutionary

XJ turned around to face the darkness from the kitchen to the living room. Her mind and body were at war. On the one hand, Brandon had her feeling warm inside. And on the other he infuriated her.

Is this dude trying to play me or what? She stormed into the living room—crashing into furniture. *I am beyond pissed. Why is my life so complicated?*

Scrambling through the pitch black hallway and into her room, she went straight for her bed. The pillows made a *whooshing* sound as she fell face first. Her day rushed back through her mind. Brandon was now the least of her worries.

What about my mom? How can I save her from a mind swipe? Torn between wanting her mother to be safe, and wanting to give up on the Revolution crap, she flipped over to face her ceiling.

Well, her mother did teach her how to survive given horrible odds. Her life was like the book, *Worse Case Scenario.* Her mother drilled her with a million, different scenarios so she knew what to do.

Most of the time. She pulled out her phone again. *Still nothing from dad. Why hasn't he called me?*

Exhaustion took over. She hadn't rested. Pulling out the provisions from the pack under her bed, she found a small flash light. *At least, I could change out of this outfit and get some rest.*

Since she had no idea what might happen, she opted to put on a pair of cargo pants, an oversized shirt, and moccasins. She grabbed her favorite pillow, an army sleeping bag, and her soft blanket. She pulled down the crawlspace stairs next to the door of her room.

Dorothy had created this space for them to hide in case of emergency. The naked eye couldn't see the latch. And the line was seamless from the outside, so it looked like a small, dry wall scratch.

Her mother had tried to make the crawlspace comfy when she was a kid. They'd hide in there for fun and games as practice. It felt like home. She'd drawn chalk drawings on the wall as a child. Tramping into the space, she crawled up and fastened the hatch. Her mother had also created eye-holes, so they could see down unnoticed.

XJ shined the light around. They hadn't hid up here in a while. She swiped at the few stray spider webs and crawled closer to the two mattresses. Dust released as she flipped one over. She sneezed and the tired weariness called for her to rest more. She got everything situated and switched out the flashlight.

Her mind wandered. *I wonder what Brandon is up to? Even though he's pissed me off, I'm really starting to crush on him hard.* Soon, she drifted off to sleep.

XJ awoke to voices. Someone was in the house. She sat up, bit her lip and tried to stop her heart from pumping so fast. Afraid to move too much, she rolled over and moved to a peep hole. CAGE officers milled around. XJ's eyes widened through the peep hole, as fear crawled up and down her spine. Would they find her?

She heard a familiar voice. "I know she's here somewhere." It was the social worker, Ms. Hughes! She tightened her internal defenses. The social worker's mind slithered out and touched hers. Sweat broke out on her forehead as she fought back fiercely.

She slammed her hand down to increase her conscious control. The social worker wriggled into her mind. XJ held her body and mind erect but she felt like a mouse inside of a cat's trap. The battle between them seemed to go on forever.

XJ felt the strong compulsion to come out of her hiding place. Her legs moved but she couldn't do anything about it. Somewhere in her consciousness she let out an angry curse. A ring-tone snapped her back into her right mind. Who would be calling her? She quietly searched around for her phone and realized that she'd left it in her bedroom.

I can't believe I was so stupid! She wiped off dusty webs and crawled around to the peep hole that was in her room.

Ms. Hughes answered, "Patterson residence." XJ strained to hear the conversation.

"I'm sorry Mr. Patterson but your ex-wife has been taken into custody, and we're currently searching for your daughter."

It's dad! XJ desperately needed to speak to him.

"Oh, no.... Don't worry. XJ will be well taken care of until you get back. She'll be in the custody of CAGE."

She heard her father's voice but couldn't make out what he said.

"Yes, your wife ... since she's a step parent, we're unable to release your daughter to her. Sorry, your daughter must go to Zone 6." Ms. Hughes was searching her room while she talked to her father.

XJ's heart dropped. How would she communicate with her father? Angry tears pushed through and XJ wiped her face with the back of her hand. She hated her life. She hated having to hide.

The social worker hung up her phone and slid it into her pocket. "XJ, I know you're here. Come out, come out wherever you are."

The social worker's compulsion slammed into her consciousness with a vengeance. How would she get out of this? She plopped down on the floor. She crossed her legs and arms. She resigned to stay in the crawl space at all costs. She refused to reveal herself. Beads of cold sweat rolled down her face. Her mouth shuttered.

She'd taken a stand. Sheer will allowed her to sit in a hyper-meditative state.

Her mother's words flooded her mind and calmed her. She began building a wall around her mind. Her head ached but she finished building an iron wall between them. She didn't know how it happened, but it kept her safe. Drenched and anxiety shaken, XJ pushed her back against the wall and waited for CAGE to leave.

After what seemed like an eternity, she heard the social worker. "I know I sensed her presence, but now there's nothing. She's gone. Did you see her out back?"

A male voice responded, "No, the offspring has not been detected."

"Well." There was shrug in the social worker's voice. "Let's wait this one out. Cut the power to the house, but leave the entrance access unmonitored. We'll catch her eventually."

XJ heard the house clear out. But to be safe, she stayed in her hiding place. With shaky hands, she took out a protein bar and ate. What was she going to do? The social worker had her phone and the house had no power. What a mess!

Finally, she couldn't take it anymore. If they captured her so be it. She had no idea how she was going to get out of this. She slid down and looked around. The house was completely empty.

The early morning sun shone through the windows. Everything seemed normal. She could hear the birds chirping as if it were just another day in the Patterson home. She moved into the living room with her hands on her hips and surveyed the disaster.

Her eyes moved towards the ring as it glistened in the sunlight. With all of the drama she'd forgotten about her grandfather. Would he still be there since CAGE had cut the power?

She ran over to the ring and put it on. Someone bear hugged her from behind. She turned around to face a CAGE officer. He'd been waiting for her. The front door crashed open.

She was surrounded.

XJ let out a yell and tried to stomp the CAGE officer in the foot. "*Let go of me*! Get your hands off me!"

A variety of arms grabbed XJ as the CAGE officers wrestled her to the ground. She kicked, punched, and yelled until her throat was raw. "Help me!"

The social worker's voice was sneaking inside her mind to calm her down. XJ erected the iron wall.

Ms. Hughes said, "This one's strong."

Suddenly, a blue light blinded everyone. A rush of adrenaline pushed into her. *What's going on now?*

She heard a mechanical voice telling her to cover her ears. She ducked and covered. A blasting tone surged throughout the room. Everyone standing grabbed their heads and passed out. XJ lay on the bottom of the pack in the fetal position with her hands over her ears.

"Over here! Hurry, doll!" Dr. Gary Leonard Kates, now a holograph, was motioning for her to enter into the wall opening.

She pushed her way out of the pack of CAGE officers. She'd almost entered the wall, but turned around and pulled her phone out of the social worker's pocket.

She rushed through the wall.

The brightness of the laboratory blinded her. It seemed as if the lab was encased in an iridescent metal. Her grandfather beckoned to her to come further inside. Another metal wall clicked into place.

He was watching the multiple computer monitors in the house. The CAGE officers and Ms. Hughes woke up. She could hear the conversations from the monitors but it was like she was in a different dimension. The social worker appeared to be trying to compel her but gave up. They finally cleared out of the house and searched her yard.

"Don't worry, doll," Gary said. "They can't find you in here." He studied them, scratching his beard. "I built this place like a fortress."

"Granddad *Kates?*" XJ asked in bewilderment. *"OMG!* How is this happening?" She walked over and touched him. She expected her hand to slide through. But he felt solid ... like flesh and blood.

She stared in disbelief. *Could this really be happening?* She didn't know what to think or do.

It seemed as if she moved from one crazy event to the other. She continued to poke at her grandfather. "You're real ... but when I saw you on the outside I could see through you." She continued to poke him.

Dr. Kates smiled. "You can stop that any time you get ready. The closer I am to my super-computer and conductor, the more real my holographic body appears. The further away ... well, you get the picture." Her grandfather swiveled his chair back towards the monitors.

XJ found a chair, plopped down like a rag doll, and rubbed her eyes with the palms of her hands. "So now you're going to tell me that you've been hiding in here—for 15 years?"

Her grandfather gazed at her intensely. At length he said, "My story is a long, complicated scientific journey. But I can certainly explain it to you in layman's terms, if you'd like."

XJ readjusted her braided ponytail. With the rubber band in her mouth, she mumbled. "The spark notes version will do." She got her hair back into a ponytail. "On second thought, just save it. I've got enough to deal with as it is."

Gary let out a defeated sigh. "For what it's worth, I'm glad to finally be able to see you as a teen. Your mother thought it best that we not tell you ... until something like this happened."

"Of course. Keep XJ in the dark. That *so* works for me." She rolled her head back and let out a scream. She stopped when she realized that CAGE was still outside; and jammed her knuckles to her lips instead.

"It's okay. Yell or scream. They won't be able to hear you." Her grandfather walked over and kissed her forehead. "Dorothy and I both know how hard this has been on you. But I promise, all will be revealed."

"Psycho babble won't work on me granddad. Mom has been filling my head up for too long."

They heard a crash on one of the monitors. XJ rushed to see. "What was *that?*"

He continued to study them on the monitor. "Hmm ... they appear to be looking for another hiding space. They certainly won't find you now. But I have something for them if they keep looking."

"Wait ... it looks like they're leaving." Her grandfather switched the monitors. They watched everyone clear out.

Feeling relieved, she slowly slid back into her chair. "So if you could've helped, why didn't you help my mom?"

"It wasn't that simple, doll." Her grandfather's image looked as if he'd suddenly gone older and grayer. "Your mother knew that you weren't prepared, and that you'd be left without the ring or knowledge of me. You're far too important for that."

"Enough with the revolutionary *bull!*"

Her grandfather swiveled around, looking angry. "Young ladies don't talk like foul-mouthed mercenaries! I think I've heard enough of your vulgarities for one day!"

XJ sucked the irritation through her teeth. *"Fine!* I'm a kid in need of her mother. Not some revolutionary in need of a cause."

Her grandfather studied her closely and scratched his beard. "XJ, you are more important than you know. We've sacrificed everything, so you and your cousins would be prepared to neutralize CAGE. This is the reason you exist."

She leaped up in a fit of anger. She didn't care anymore. Tears streamed down her face as she gestured. "Are you kidding me? Unbelievable! *Un fr ... ea ... king* believable."

Her grandfather dropped back and surveyed her from a distance. His manner made her feel like a lab rat. *Why does everyone want something from me? I'm N-O-T a revolutionary.*

She just wanted to be a normal teenager. Was that so hard for everyone to accept?

Chapter 16

"The less a GEP knows about the inner workings of CAGE, the more he trusts those who hold the power; And the more he trusts those in power, the more likely he'll become their victim."

—Dr. Gary Leonard Kates, Revolutionary

Her grandfather massaged the gray beard on his face again. He wasn't responding to her tears. XJ wanted to storm out of the lab, but she wasn't sure if CAGE had really gone. She felt pissed off at the both of them.

Did dad know too? Why was I left out? Why does everyone want me to be a revolutionary?

She slid back into the chair. Everything took hold of her and she felt overwhelmed. She wanted a better life for herself. Her grandfather walked over and rubbed her back.

"I'm so sorry, XJ ... I'm so sorry." Gary repeated softly. "We never meant for any of this to happen." His soothing voice faded in and out. She finally quieted and a sense of relief flooded her. She wiped her tears from her face with the back of her arm.

"So, what am I missing?"

Dr. Kates straightened his back. "Well, I certainly don't miss the up and down hormones of a teen girl. Let's see. Where do I begin?"

"Why don't you start with how I can help my mom?" XJ folded her arms tight. Her stomach jumped up and down.

"Dorothy uncovered some important information when she went undercover—information that got her in a bind."

"What? Would you stop being so secretive already?"

He cleared his throat and graciously continued. "In her mission to locate your cousins, she came across material that suggested that CAGE was creating a mechanism by which to control all genetically-enhanced persons." He paused.

XJ blurted out, "So are you saying mom uncovered a plan for CAGE to take over the world?"

Dr. Kates gave a flat smile. "There are no games here, doll. This is for real. Look for yourself." He pulled up documents on a viewing screen. XJ pulled the screen closer and examined them.

She put her hands behind her head and eased back into her seat. "This proves that she's innocent! This is what I've been looking for! *Proof*—proof that I can give to that reporter, Fitch!"

"*No*, XJ. I highly advise against that. People like him are not to be trusted...." Her grandfather tried to explain.

She leapt up in frustration and pointed at the screen. "No, you hold on! I've been sitting here on pins and needles, trying to figure out how I can get my mom out of this, and here is my answer."

Dr. Kates settled back again in his examination mode. He said, "Well, it's not like I can stop you. But before you share this, you need to know more about your cousins and how you all were designed to dismantle CAGE."

XJ heard nothing. She'd become fixated on the CAGE documents and freeing her mother. She took out her drive and loaded the documents. Her mind and heart raced. She could give these to Fitch! He would use them to put pressure on CAGE to free her mother. She was liking the idea more and more.

She heard her grandfather rattling on about destiny and long, lost family members. But her soul focused on freeing her mother. She slipped the drive in her pocket and asked, "Grandad is there a back exit to this lab? I've got something to do."

XJ's thumb played with the small drive in her pocket, while she rode on the MARTA bus. Her body lurched at each bus stop. She was drawing closer and closer to freeing her mother, and returning to the somewhat normal life she'd had before. She wanted nothing to do with the stupid Revolution. In fact, she felt like going far, far away to college to get away from the mess.

"Downtown Decatur next exit...," The bus driver's voice announced. The normalcy of riding the bus versus listening to her holographic grandfather struck her. She didn't understand what he was rattling on about—distant cousins, and the fact that they'd all been enhanced to become a super weapon. It was all too much for her to deal with!

Apprehension filled her as the bus pulled up to her exit. *This has to work! CAGE will have to let mom go after this!*

She marched with determination to Fitch's office. On the phone, he sounded excited about working with her story. She could already see the headlines: *Dorothy Kates Patterson Freed. CAGE rescinds charges.*

XJ put her fist up in the air. "YES!" *Finally, a win for me and my family!*

Feeling the morning sun on her face, XJ smiled and opened the door to the *GEP Daily Post*. She felt relaxed as she walked up. After the skinny, little receptionist gave XJ a cappuccino with whipped cream, she showed her to Fitch's office.

She sipped her drink on the way to the office, puffed her chest out and swaggered down the hall.

Smiling, she greeted the reporter with a warm handshake. "Mr. Fitch, it's so good to see you again! I'm happy that we're working together to share the truth about my mom."

"Sit down, please." He motioned to the chair. "This promises to be the story of the century."

XJ took a sip of cappuccino. She almost felt normal. She slid the drive out of her pocket and onto his desk. This nightmare was over. She could feel it. A warm glow spread through her. Soon Dorothy would be home, and she'd convince her to give up the Revolution and become a normal mom.

XJ felt something pierce her skin. She dropped the cappuccino on the floor, slapped her neck and pulled out a dart. Her eyes widened. Suddenly she was starring into the barrel of a gun. Her body jerked. Her head swam.

The room spun as she took a full face dive into Fitch's desk.

Chapter 17

"GEPs are poor creatures. They are half-human and half-gods traveling in a dangerous genetically enhanced direction. God help us. They must be controlled."

—President, Humans United

Brandon couldn't get XJ out of his mind. All night he thought about holding her, keeping her safe and caressing her. It was weird. He'd never felt this way about any girl, but XJ did it for him. Would she ever speak to him again?

He smacked himself upside the head. *Stupid! I'm so stupid! Why did I have to tell her that I wanted the story?*

The sun streaked through his window as he rolled over. He wondered if XJ had a good night. Sliding out of his bed, he tramped to his bathroom and got into the shower. The hot water stung his back and hair.

He kept thinking about her as he felt his manhood rise. He hadn't had a boner like this *ever*. This girl had him turned inside out. What was he going to do?

He finished soaping up. He stepped out of the shower and dried himself off. His mind kept running a mile a second. What should he do next? How would he prove that Fitch was bad news? He knew there was more to all of this. He needed more information. He had no idea how to reveal Fitch's deception.

He continued to get himself dressed. He knew exactly what he had to do. Instead of breaking into Fitch's computer, he would take a different approach. He needed to get to school to meet with the Young Revolutionaries. He finished dressing and headed down the long hall to the back kitchen. He preferred eating away from his father.

At first, it had upset him that Todd wasn't there when he woke up from the incident with Fitch. But now that he felt better he had no desire to see him.

He rounded the corner and slammed into his dad. *Christ! Where did he come from?*

His dad backed up. "I see you're doing better."

Brandon's stomach was tied into knots. "I'm fine," he mumbled and continued towards the kitchen.

Todd blocked his path. "What were you doing in Fitch's office?"

Brandon backed up. *Why does he always make me feel like a five year old?* "What does it matter to you?" he said angrily, trying to push passed Todd.

His father was immovable. "While you're in my house, and under my rule, you WILL answer my questions!"

Brandon shrunk back against the wall. Should he tell him anything? *No. I don't owe him any explanation. Did I ever get an explanation about my mother? In fact, why isn't he putting the pressure on CAGE to find out more about mom's murder?*

He wouldn't go easily or quietly. A cold hatred filled his eyes, "I won't tell you. My sole purpose in life is to make sure you *pay*. So if I have to snoop into your business to find a traitor then I'll do it. Isn't that what your business is all about trading the freedom of all GEPs?"

Brandon watched his dad's shoulders collapse and felt elated. *Good! Glad I made you uncomfortable.* "Can I go now? I have to get to school."

Todd hesitated, but just then his cell phone went off. He gave Brandon an exasperated look. "Miller here..., yes...." His dad broke off his conversation and pointed at Brandon. "This isn't over young man!"

Brandon whispered under his breath, "Yeah, I know. You've got business to take care of." He bypassed Todd, walked into the kitchen and picked up a freshly made breakfast sandwich to go.

He had better things to do than think that his dad gave a damn about him or who'd murdered his mom. He munched on his sandwich as he made his way to the garage. He slid into his Mustang and floored it to school.

Brandon walked distracted through the sea of brown, Asian, and white faces in the hallway. He focused on texting XJ's phone. She wasn't responding. He made a quick exasperated rake through his hair.

Man! I messed up royally this time.

She wouldn't even take his calls. He knew that she'd been upset with him. But he'd begun to believe that there was a feeling growing between them amidst all the drama.

He walked to his next class giving some half-high fives and receiving second glances from others. He could care less. He needed to figure out how to get XJ to talk to him again—convince her that Fitch wasn't on the up and up, before she gave any information.

He had to meet up with the Young Revolutionaries to brainstorm a plan of action. Hopefully, they'd give him something to work with. He could run by her house after school to pitch his idea, and make sure she was okay.

Brandon settled in his seat and pulled out his folder. The class was eerily quiet but he wasn't focused on them. He heard a small gasp of disbelief from a girl who sat in front of him. Everyone started whispering, and watching the news on a small hand-held device.

Aggravated, he turned. They were watching the breaking news.

"Just in. XJ Patterson, the granddaughter of the slain GEP activist, Dr. Gary Leonard Kates, has just been taken in for questioning by CAGE: the small governmental branch that regulates Genetically Enhanced Persons. It appears that she was in possession of stolen classified documents. Stay tuned for more details from Regional Director, Nadia Stillwater, in her press conference."

A shocked *F-bomb* rolled off his tongue in slow motion.

Rose perfume assaulted his nose and a pale arm slid down the front of his chest. Heather took both of her hands, squeezed his cheeks together and forced him to face her devilish grin.

"Oh, Brandon. I wish you'd look that way for me. All torn up about your little jungle bunny?" She puckered her lips for dramatic appeal.

Brandon was not impressed. He jerked her hands from his face. "What do you want, Heather?"

Chapter 18

"The development of a human weapon against CAGE is inevitable. It must be done by any means or sacrifice, if we hope to be free."

—Dr. Gary Leonard Kates, Revolutionary Meeting

She rolled over on the smelly old mattress and threw up in the holding cell toilet. XJ's head exploded as her stomach heaved. She crumbled back onto the stinky mattress and placed her arm on her forehead. Her breath came in short gasps. It took her several minutes to center herself, as she thought of what happened.

One minute she was happily sharing what she knew with Fitch ... and the next she was staring down the barrel of a gun.

Her body shivered, as she remembered that CAGE officers had shot her with a tranquilizer gun in his office. Her last memory was of Fitch's triumphant smile, as she toppled over.

XJ sat up on the edge of the bed. "That jerk set me up." She sighed deeply, and looked around the empty cell.

She tried to stand, but her legs started to wobble so she slid back down. The bed squeaked. She slumped her shoulders and wiped her eyes. Her body shuddered more as she looked around. The cell smelled like urine and torture. Everything held a drab dull green haze from the flickering light.

Her mother's soothing voice wafted through her mind. *"They take you to a holding cell, first, for hours to let you sweat it out and then the questions begin. Don't let them trick you. Be silent, no matter how much it hurts."*

Was she becoming a revolutionary? The thought sickened her. She rolled over again, and just made it to the toilet to barf up more of her stomach. She wiped her mouth. Fitch had been her last hope. She wanted to use the press to pressure CAGE to free her mother. Peacefully.

But now the headlines probably read like something else ... *OMG, I've become my revolutionary mother!*

The revelation crashed into her. She bit her bottom lip and tried to stop from shaking. *What I am supposed to do now?*

She should have listened to Brandon. She'd dreamed about him. The moment they shared together still made her feel warm inside.

The girl scooted down on the squeaky bed, and rubbed the spot where they shot her. She felt violated, confused and hurt. Her mother was gone. She closed her eyes: determined.

If what her Mom said was true, she'd be facing something terrible and she needed to rest as well as erect mental, iron walls. She squeezed her eyes shut and pushed back until she touched the cold walls.

Her mental work had begun.

XJ dozed in and out of sleep, for what seemed like hours; until she heard the jail cell bars grate open. Ms. Hughes sauntered into her cell. She sat up and squeezed her nails into her palms. The bars smashed shut behind the social worker.

Hughes gave her a gold tooth grin, and stood like a hungry lion ready to battle.

Inside XJ's mind she heard, *"So you weren't able to escape me after all."*

She focused on erecting her mental iron walls. But the compulsion jerked her mind and she felt her legs twitch. She leaned back and grimaced. Cold perspiration rolled down her back. Her body was moving without her permission!

A nauseating, rolling sensation swept through her and she used everything within to fight back. Her nerves were scraped raw. She wrestled with the urge to scream. She had to focus.

Hughes continued her mental assault—sending wave after wave of compulsion to try and manipulate the girl's body without her permission. The two threw mental blows back and forth, until XJ thought she'd crumble or her brain would cave-in, then the struggle subsided a little.

"You little tramp!" The social worker sneered. "You won't get away this time—there's nowhere to run or hide!" *How could I keep this woman from controlling me?*

"I did nothing wrong!" XJ grunted with intensity. "I'm just a kid that's trapped in an impossible situation!"

She continued to use singular focus. The mental assault picked up again, but this time the wave of thoughts were piercing her mind. XJ choked—beginning to drown inside her own psyche. Her spirit trembled. She couldn't catch her breath.

The life was being soaked out of her.

Down, she thought, *calm down*. Hughes began to compel her to answer questions. XJ bit down on her quivering lip.

"I'll let you to drown in your own bodily fluids, if you don't tell me what I want to know!" Hughes' words thundered within the room and XJ's mind. "Did your mother give you the information that you shared with the reporter?"

Her mouth opened. But she was able to keep the words from spilling out. The mental swarm attacked, but washed over XJ. A flat smile curled about her lips, as her eyes popped open. She wouldn't tell her a thing.

But could she lie?

"I ... have ... no ... idea what you're ... talking about!" XJ gritted her teeth and exerted an intense concentration to keep the truth from rolling out.

The mental assault stopped. Her mind cleared and she sat up. The social worker looked *pissed*. "Remove her and place her in the chamber!"

She gasped ... she'd focused on the social worker and didn't realize that she was surrounded by CAGE officers. Each officer took one of her limbs and dragged her down the hall—Ms. Hughes laughing manically as XJ tried to fight them off.

They slammed her beleaguered body onto a lab gurney. Her eyes turned gray, as she used her telekinetic abilities to stop them from strapping her down. She kicked, punched, and bit her attackers. Hughes had wore her out mentally. Her abilities fizzled. Her entire body ached. She still fought—hard.

How much more of this could she take? Anger boiled in her gut as they secured her legs, then her arms. Her body shook as the realization took hold. It was the cold emptiness in the officers' eyes. They would restrain her or do whatever was necessary to take her out.

She cried, screamed, pulled at her restraints. Then her heart dropped and a dizzying depression took root inside her mind. *Maybe I should tell them so they'll let me go!* They wheeled her down a long dark hall.

She swiveled her head in different directions. "Where are you taking *me?*" she screamed like a mad woman. Her response was the sound of the wheels scraping across the floor.

"What do you want from me?" Her lungs burned from exhaustion and stress. The gurney halted and they parked her next to a wall. XJ heard the boots of the CAGE officers march away in unison. Her body shuddered. Tears rolled down her cheeks and face.

Brandon must think I'm an idiot by now! He was right about Fitch! She couldn't even wipe her face, so she turned her head to wipe the tears on the hard gurney.

"Crying won't help," a plain, matter-of-fact, voice called from the other side of the hallway.

"Who's there?" XJ asked, squinting. A silhouette of a young woman, about her own age, came into focus. Like her, she was strapped down.

"I've been here for six months and I swear that crying won't help," the girl said in the same flat, emotionless voice. "It just gets worse each day."

"Do you know where they're taking me?"

"From the looks of things, you're on your way to the chamber." The girl droned on as if she were talking about crossing the street. "Your best bet is to tell them what they want to know. But don't tell them too soon 'cause they'll get suspicious."

"So, what do I do? I don't have any more information." XJ lied.

"Well ... if I were you I would try to black out," the young woman said, "I've been here for what seems like forever and I don't even know what they want outta me. I've resorted to making up stuff so they'll leave me alone. By the way, my name is Amber...."

XJ took a deep breath, "My name is XJ ... XJ Patterson. I just want to go home."

"Highly unlikely. Once CAGE has you, you're in for good. I should know. *Shh...!*" Amber lowered her voice to a scared hushed whisper. "Here they come! It was good to meet you, XJ. I'm sure we'll meet again in Zone 6. That's where we all end up...."

She heard the CAGE officer's boots tramping in and her gurney was back in motion. Glancing over to get a better look at Amber, she saw that besides her lighter skin color, they seemed to have similar body builds and features.

XJ rolled her head back to the center and watched the ceiling tiles pass across her vision. She'd have to put up a fake fight, at first; and then pretend to be defeated. She'd give them a big fat lie to get out of this.

Her mother had trained her to ward off these types of interrogations. But was she ready for what was ahead?

Chapter 19

"GEPS suffer at the hands of CAGE. One day CAGE will suffer at the hands of GEPS. It's inevitable."
—Dorothy Kates-Patterson, Revolutionary Meeting

The guards rolled XJ into the chamber like executioners. The slow steady movement drove her insane. She stretched her body and wiggled her hands and feet. Tightened down and trapped, her nerves were raw. This certainly was not what she'd expected.

Her mind wandered into a daydream where she fantasized about what should have happened.

The dream calmed her down. The paparazzi surrounded her with questions about how she single-handedly brought down CAGE. They were forced to release her mother. And she announced at the end of her news conference, her desire to enter the Miss GEP High School Pageant with Brandon as her escort.

The wheels of the gurney dragged her back into the moment and she trembled.

"Excuse me," She squeaked out, "Can I get some water?"

They ignored her.

She gained a little more confidence, "Can a sista' please get a drink of water?"

The gurney stopped, and a man dressed in a white lab coat approached. "I'm Dr. Winfred Robinson. This will help minimize the pain." The doctor adjusted his glasses and smiled as he took out a syringe like tube, rolled up her sleeve and jammed her arm with drugs.

Her mouth went dry. Her body stiffened. She couldn't move. It was as if she was paraplegic. The only things she could move were her eye lids, and her mouth ... but very slowly.

Unable to speak above a soft whisper, she pleaded. "Please, please don't do this to me."

The doctor touched her arm and gave her a consoling look. "It'll be over soon."

They moved the gurney into another room, where she was further restrained. A single tear rolled down her face.

How could they do this to me?

The guards lifted her head and placed it into a metal brace with a microphone hanging over her head. Then they took out industrial strength straps and further tightened and secured her body. If she'd had any feelings left, she would have sobbed. Her mind moved a mile per second. But she couldn't concentrate. Her limbs sat lifeless.

A whispered cry escaped her lips. The guards rolled her into a chamber and attached each gurney wheel into a locked, docking station. Claustrophobic terror gripped XJ as the guards left the chamber. The sound of the door clicking into a dead lock left her in silence.

She lay there for what seemed like a scary eternity. She went deeper into her psyche, and focused on memories of the fun times she'd spent as a child....

"If you're happy and you know it, clap your hands. If you're happy and you know it clap your hands." XJ held on to the vision of her mother showing her how to play this game, while they were at a revolutionary meeting.

Red, blue, and green strobe lights flickered. The flashing picked up pace until the lights abused her senses. The drugs kept her from closing her eyes. The stimulus forced her mind to go wild, as the front and back ends of the chamber began to move opposite the direction of the gurney.

XJ's mind went into a psychedelic haze. She screamed until she was hoarse, as everything swirled. The entire gurney—with her on it—began to spin at a breakneck speed. Her brain told her that she needed to throw up, but the drugs held everything down. She was spun round ... and round ... and round....

Then, she felt Hughes' presence, like a slithering reptile. "Now, you're ready to tell. What's your secret, little XJ?" Her sinister laughter echoed throughout the chamber.

Hughes' compulsion moved her mouth, but XJ fought hard to keep it in. What could she do? She couldn't move and the spinning was driving her insane. She focused on Brandon's lips and the softness of his kiss. He'd held her so gently and he felt safe. If she could get out of this, she would get closer to him.

I never had a guy like him before....

Her whispered, scratchy voice echoed in the microphone and room. "I don't know anything else. Please let me go. I told you eveything." The room sped up and the lights moved even faster....

What lie can I tell them?

Then she sensed the social worker telepathically igniting a phobia inside her mind. XJ could feel poisonous snakes and spiders skittering underneath her skin. Extreme madness overtook her. She screamed in terror.

XJ had had enough. She wouldn't allow them to continue to torture her. In a hazy attack, she pushed all of the compulsion out of her mind. She thought she heard the social worker shriek, but she couldn't tell—all she knew was that the phobia disappeared while the room continued to spin.

Her mind spun. She faded in and out so much that she couldn't tell where she was or what was happening. Then she went to a quiet place within herself where Brandon's warm embrace soothed her while her conscious mind crashed on top of itself and faded into technicolor.

Chapter 20

"When I want to know what GEPs think, I ask myself."
—Nadia Stillwater

Heather was ecstatic about the deal she'd made with Brandon. He'd agreed to escort her to the Miss GEP High School Pageant. If she brought him XJ. She smiled. She never intended to do that, but she could use it to make him do what she wanted.

Brandon will see that jungle bunny again, but it's gonna cost him. Her smile widened, and she sat up taller in her car seat. *Brandon does love me!* She knew she could either control him or convince him to be hers.

Either way, she was one step closer to making him hers again.

Her brain clattered. *"Ouch!"* She yelled and swerved her car into a restricted parking spot. *Thump, thump, thump* pounded against the front of her skull.

The other Heather pushed hard to get out. "Brandon doesn't love you! Saskia loves you!"

Heather engaged in a mental battle with herself. Her head pounded. Reality hammered. She passed out on the steering wheel and came to with a grinding headache.

"Leave me *alone!*" Heather rested her forehead back on the steering wheel. "This is my time!" she shrieked. "You didn't win! *I* did! Go away!"

Heather barreled back deeper inside the space of her mind that kept the personalities divided. The thin wall threatened to rupture, but she held it up. She would have her victory she would not be denied.

The brain thumping subsided and Heather was back in control. Her legs swam like Jello and her hands shook. But she was back. She pushed up in her car seat, pulled the rear view mirror towards her and laughed.

"I'm still in control! I win!" She wiped the sweat from her forehead. "I'll show you." She reached behind and pulled out her hot pink purse. Her phone fell out. Had she sent a text? She couldn't remember. She fished out the white pills and gulped two without water.

She cracked her neck and craned it around to relieve the tightness. Heather smiled wickedly at her reflection. She dug deeper into her purse and pulled out make-up. After puckering, pinching and pruning she made herself look marvelous.

She pushed open the car door and got out. Heather took a deep, clearing breath. It felt good to be in control. The cool spring wind blew her pink scarf. She knew her rose perfume would tickle the nose of anyone close.

She stood taller. Heather knew she was sexy in her hot pink, high-heeled lace-up boots, white mini-skirt, and hot pink blouse with form-fitting blazer. She exuded confidence as her blond curls bounced. She secretly relished the hungry glances from the guards.

Inside her mind she said, *See how beautiful I am? They love me.*

The other Heather was silent. Maybe she'd given up. Maybe the medicine had worked. Maybe she could finally be herself.

Heather strolled into the restricted area. She rounded the corner and collided with Saskia. Before she knew it, warm arms encircled her. Startled, Heather dropped her defenses and relaxed into the deep embrace.

Saskia was everything that she needed. Heather's lips touched the woman's instinctively. A part of her fought her body's reaction. She couldn't stop.

Heather opened her mouth and heart to Saskia's hungry kiss. Warmth spread throughout her body. She reciprocated ferociously—her entire body inflamed. She wanted to fall into Saskia's bottomless kiss.

Heather's two personalities collided: one thoroughly enjoying the loving kiss; and the other repulsed by it.

The one inside yelled, *Oh, God! What are you* thinking? *Stop! Break it off!*

But it was too late. The Heather that adored Saskia took over. *Shut up. I love her.*

Heather sunk deeper into Saskia's embrace. She was starving for her touch. This was the only place that she wanted to be.

Suddenly Heather's head and body yanked backward, shattering the kiss. Her breath came in fast gulps. She frowned as cool air separated her and Saskia.

Heather balled up her fist. "How dare you...!" Her shoulders slumped as she realized that she faced her mother.

"What the hell are you doing?" Her mother yelled. And before Heather could step out of the way, the impact of the smack rattled her teeth. Heather's face burned. The tears threatened to fall but Heather held them in.

This Heather was pissed at her mother and didn't care what she did. "Why did you hit me?"

Her mother's face said it all. Nadia grabbed Heather and dragged her down the hall to her office. Before she knew it, Heather was hurled into a chair like a rag doll. Her stomach lurched. Her heart drummed. She wanted to fight her mother. She hated her. Heather bit back the hatred.

"You've never lived up to my expectations!" I'm going to replace you. Since you're adopted, it'll be easy. Xavier and I will have a baby."

Heather could tell that her mother wanted a response. She sat stiff and didn't move. Her abilities went wild. Her hands shook. She was very close to turning on the hunter part of herself. Her vision turned red.

"Who am I talking to now?" Nadia moved closer to Heather and pulled her chin up. "Who are you? Tell me or I'll make you hurt bad!"

This Heather knew who her mother wanted, but didn't care. Inside her mind she said, *I know who you want* ... she smiled, *but she's not available.*

What came out was, "I'm here, mother. I'm just trying to give you what you want." Her stomach twisted at the lie, but her abilities ramped up. She watched her mother closely, her abilities making everything stand-out, and zeroed in on Nadia's gloved hands. How could she stop her from removing her gloves?

"So, you like girls, huh? All those beautiful young men I've given you. Such a waste."

Heather's stomach did flip-flops, with hazy memories of all the boys that her mother made her get close to. Made her have sex with. Made her screw them over. And she was sickened.

Heather wanted to scream, to cry. She lied. "I—I don't like girls. I was just practicing; you misunderstood."

Her mother released a deep, irritated breath. "You don't fool me. I *know* which one you are. Bring *MY* Heather back now."

Those hands came out of her gloves *fast*. Heather tried to dodge the evil touch, but couldn't move swiftly enough. Her mother's ability pulsed throughout her body. The pain spread with deadly purpose.

Let me out! the other Heather yelled. *You're going to get us killed. I told you to leave that stupid girl alone!*

She let her out.

Sweat poured down Heather's back. "It's me! It's me mother!" she screamed. "Don't do this!" The pain receded, and Nadia pulled Heather by the collar so that their faces were almost kissing.

"Where's Brandon?" Her mother asked through clinched teeth.

"I've kept tabs on him." Heather looked away to avoid direct eye contact with her mother.

"When's the last time you had sex with him? Don't lie." Nadia's blue eyes pierced her soul.

Heather shifted uncomfortably. She bowed her spine, trying to put space between them. "You know we haven't done it since the summer." She braced herself for the slap or tingling pain.

Her mother pulled her closer and she smashed her eyes shut. She couldn't catch her breath.

"It's XJ isn't it? You let her steal him like Dorothy stole Xavier from me." Heather could hear the disgust in her mother's voice. "I never understood how they were able to mate," Nadia went on. "I was Xavier's rightful mate but Dorothy stole him. I won him back, in the end."

Heather had heard this so many times so she played along. "XJ won't steal Brandon from me." She let the words slide from her mouth and squirmed back so she could be free from her mother's grip.

"I gave you a mission and you failed me. I won't tolerate this much longer." Her mother slipped her gloves back on.

"I won't fail you."

Her mother cleared her throat. "That Miller boy is a part of my plan. You and he must mate. You must produce an offspring. His money and pedigree are a part of my plan." She leaned in close. "You won't waste that pretty face of yours. You will give me what I want."

"I'll convince him he loves me. I have a plan." This Heather believed every word. "I won't let that little jungle bunny take him."

Her mother folded her arms. "What is this plan? Does it involve putting my step daughter in Zone 6? I'd like to be done with her. I want Xavier to only focus on our child when it's time."

Heather was beside herself with joy and she let it show. "You'll be rid of XJ. I promise. With my plan, Zone 6 won't be a strong enough punishment."

Her mother studied her closely; and then sat back up and pointed her finger. "Bring me that Miller boy or I'll disown you. I'll put *you* in Zone 6."

"You don't have to worry mother. I can handle this. We may not share the same blood, but you've taught me well. Brandon will be mine ... in the end."

Heather stood up, straightened her outfit and sashayed out of her mother's office.

Heather strolled into the chamber room. She'd heard screams, but it was Hughes who was scratching like a dog without a flea collar.

"What are you doing?" She allowed the arrogant disgust to slither out of her mouth.

The social worker looked dumbfounded, as she flicked off fake bugs. "We almost have her ready for you, Miss Stillwater."

"Ri-i-ght." Heather moved towards the chamber window and peered in. "Looks like my step sister is more powerful than you thought. Release her."

Hughes stopped flicking. *"Release* her? I'm just getting started!"

Heather's vision turned red, and she allowed the hunter to show. "Did you hear me? I *said* release her now."

"As you wish, but I will discuss this with your mother." Heather didn't care what the woman did. "Fine. Have her ready in an hour."

Heather smiled. She was close to having Brandon on a tight leash. He wouldn't get away now. She spun on her heels, and tramped to the door. Once outside, she texted Brandon and told him to meet her.

She'd give him his little jungle bunny and control him, so that he'd have no choice but to be hers.

Chapter 21

"Freedom costs, especially for GEPs."
—Dorothy Kates-Patterson

Brandon touched the trunk of his Mustang and used his ability to turn on the camera inside his back window. He ruffled his hair and stood up straight. He so badly wanted to help XJ. He was sure that she'd work with him now and he wanted to get some good footage.

He cleared his throat. "This is Brandon Miller reporting for Revolution TV. I'm outside the Regional CAGE facility. Why am I here?" Brandon's voice squeaked and his face flushed. He bit his lip and cleared his throat again. He couldn't understand why this segment was so hard. He worked at it some more.

"Why am I here? To pick up the granddaughter of slain GEP activist, Dr. Gary Leonard Kates. Stop!" Brandon jumped up and down in aggravation. *When the heck are they coming out anyway?*

Brandon closed his eyes and refocused. "XJ was taken against her will and has been held by CAGE for several hours. Why would CAGE take this innocent teenage girl, anyway?"

Ugh! This is awful. XJ deserves better than this.

His stomach lurched when he thought about what CAGE might have done to her. And he was willing to do what it took to keep her safe—even make a pact with Heather. Brandon stretched his neck. Heather had him by the balls with this agreement. But he'd been trying to figure out how to get out of it and save XJ.

His phone buzzed. He pulled out his phone and read the text. *Bring XJ to the attached location when she's free. Brockman.*

Brandon scratched his head. *How'd Brockman even know where I am and what I'm up to?*

The older man kept tabs on him more than his dad. He scanned the area around the gate, trying to make himself inconspicuous. He respected him. Where Todd made him feel worthless, Brockman made him feel important. And unlike his dad, he respected Brandon's opinions.

Brandon put his phone away and got back to his story. "XJ Patterson is a bright, wonderful, young woman who has survived many odds. Her family has had to sacrifice...."

Brandon felt Heather's arms sneak up and snake around his body. He jumped out of the way.

"It's about time!" Brandon tried to put some distance between them, but she kept moving forward. How was she able to sneak up on him anyway? Was he that busy?

"Here's your little jungle bunny!" Heather spat. "You might want to take her and go before they change their minds!"

"Don't you think that jungle bunny joke is getting old?" He turned from her, smoothed XJ's face and positioned himself so he could pick her up.

He gently eased XJ's body out of the vehicle and carried her like a precious flower. Once inside his Mustang, he made sure her seat belt was fastened.

Heather was on top of him when he turned around. Brandon's stomach soured. She smashed her lips on his, and tried to give him an x-rated death kiss. His body gave a negative reaction, but he tried to please her ... his return kiss was faint-hearted, apprehensive.

She didn't notice and beamed while she had him in her snare. "I know you like it. I felt you kiss me back. It was like what we used to be...."

Brandon regarded her blandly. "I've got to get XJ someplace safe. Call me later."

He could hear the excitement in Heather's voice, "You're *mine*. You're all mine. Remember our deal."

This is gonna blow up in my face, but at least XJ is alright.

As he moved to his side of the car, Heather smacked his butt. "Take care of the jungle bunny, then come back to momma."

Brandon let out an exasperated breath and couldn't move fast enough. He could feel Heather's stalker, red-eyed look as she leapt into the CAGE vehicle and took off in a maddened spin out.

Rushing to get himself and XJ out of there, he connected his phone to his dash and added the directions that he'd received from Brockman.

He looked over at the unconscious XJ. *She looks like she been through hell!*

Worry spread throughout his body, but he pushed it away. He wanted to lash out at CAGE and wondered how could he use Revolution TV to bring them all down.

Brandon drove them both to safety.

Chapter 22

"Perfect love makes us stronger and more willing to take chances that lead to freedom."
—Dr. Gary Leonard Kates

XJ drifted in and out of sleep. She felt warm arms around her body and smelled inviting male cologne. It permeated her entire body. The embrace and scent awakened deep feelings. The strong male hands caressed her hair and face.

If she was still being tortured at CAGE, this was the best she'd experienced. Maybe she'd gone completely mad in the chamber? She snuggled and he held her more tightly.

Her conscious mind woke up. He'd reciprocated? Where was she and who was caressing her? Her stomach flip flopped and her eyes popped open. Startled and out of sorts she gazed deep into Brandon's sexy blue eyes.

"OMG!" She screamed. XJ jumped back in embarrassment and inflamed longing.

"It's okay ... you're safe now." Brandon responded gently. "CAGE can't find you here."

Questions slammed into XJ's mind and out of her mouth. "How did I get here? Where am I? Am I dead?"

Brandon's face so close to hers, sparked an urge inside of her. "Calm down ... you're safe."

His voice sounded reassuring, but she needed to put some distance between the two of them. In her mind, there were too many reasons why they shouldn't be together.

He's white.

I'm black.

He's rich.

I'm poor.

He's a revolutionary.

I'm not ... at least I don't think I am.

It's illegal.

He's not my acceptable mate-designation type.

A relationship between the two of them that yielded any offspring, would certainly wind up a pickled aborted fetus in Zone 6. XJ shuddered.

She felt exposed. Vulnerable. "Is there a restroom here?" She scanned the room and realized that they were in some sort of motel—they were in the bed together! XJ jumped and almost fell on the floor, but Brandon caught her.

"Be careful, you're going to hurt yourself!" His voice calmed her as he pulled her gently back on the bed. The touch ignited a flushed spark. His touch, stare, and concern proved too much for XJ. She bolted for the restroom and slammed the door.

She heard Brandon through the door, but couldn't get her mind together. This was too sudden and thoughts swirled. Her life was a mess. She washed her face and looked at herself in the mirror.

"Are you alright? Do you feel sick?" Brandon's words assaulted the door. He sounded worried.

"I'll be out in a minute...." XJ washed out her mouth with the nearest mouthwash and tried to pull herself together. She still couldn't believe it.

"I'm just trying to make sure this is real. How'd I get away from CAGE?"

"I made a deal to get you out of there. You're safe." She heard his forehead thump the door as he took deep breaths.

Emotions tore through XJ as the memories flooded. She'd made a terrible mistake in trusting Fitch and CAGE took her. But she thought she'd never get out. She thought she'd never have a chance to apologize to Brandon. She thought that he would have abandoned her.

She opened the door and saw Brandon standing there, wanting to help keep her safe. Tears gushed and he pulled her into his arms.

"I'm so sorry, Brandon! I'm so sorry...!" The words flooded out of her mouth in a deep sob. "I was wrong to trust Fitch."

"It's okay," he told her while caressing her hair. "At least you're safe now and that's all that matters." His strokes moved from her hair to her face.

Tears dried up and an urge awakened inside her. His tender touch wiped away her tears and his mouth moved close to hers. Passion ignited. XJ found herself in a deep, greedy kiss that was both wet and warm. Her body reacted from the top of her head to the bottom of her soul.

Her stomach turned somersaults as the kiss brought frenzied satisfaction. She didn't want to break the kiss.

But this can't be real! She couldn't allow herself to get involved with Brandon no matter how much she enjoyed his touch. XJ pulled back....

And her body felt the absent cold.

Chapter 23

"I can't trust anybody in the Revolution over 30."

—XJ Patterson, Granddaughter of Dr. Gary Leonard Kates

Brandon couldn't stand the distance between them. He pulled her back into his embrace. She made him feel eager, excited, and ready. He'd had other girls—gone all the way many times.

But he'd never felt like this. He was caught between being her protector and complete infatuation. His longing ignited....

He would *have* her. He reached for her sweet, pecan brown face. Feather gentle, he placed his lips on hers and their kiss exploded again in a hot, passionate, spicy frenzy. He didn't care about designation types or racial differences.

Brandon didn't care about any of it. He decided that XJ would be his mate—even if he had to dismantle CAGE single-handedly. Her body softened into his caress. He had a boner out of this world.

His mind raced, then slowed for XJ. Was she a virgin? He'd never heard any rumors about her. He'd have to be extra special, then. He would never treat her like he'd treated Heather.

The hotness from the kissing and warm caresses took on a rhythmic tone as Brandon led them towards to the bed. Without breaking the kiss, he eased down on the bed and XJ's body came close to straddling his. He wanted to touch every part of her. He fell deep into her dark brown eyes. He gently guided her deeper into his warmth.

Brandon slid his hand across her neck, touching her pain reducing chip. The small electric pulse made him more excited. The kiss grew deeper and more enjoyable. Finally, he had XJ on the bed and he flipped her over, so that he was on top. The heat in her eyes engulfed him and his manhood hardened.

He *had* to have her and wanted to ask if he could.... He wanted to move to the next level ... wanted to love her deeper. He lowered himself and tasted her mouth. She reciprocated hungrily. *What can I do? Should I ask if she's a virgin?*

He began to move his hands down the rest of her body. She gasped softly and deepened his kiss and caress.... There was a thunderous knock at the door. Now was not the time!

"Brandon, you in there?"

It's Brockman.

"Yeah...." Brandon sucked in his breath. "We're here; just a sec."

Brandon waited for XJ to head for the restroom and then answered the door. Brockman pushed passed him.

"Were you guys sleeping or something?" Brockman asked. Brandon shifted positions and motioned for him to sit at the nearby table.

"XJ was exhausted, She's been a little emotional." Brandon's voice trailed as he thought about his rock hard boner. He was so glad that he was wearing jogging pants. When XJ slipped out of the restroom, he felt his face flush.

"Ah XJ, there you are! So good to see you again." Brockman extended his hand.

"Brockman?" She sounded incensed. "What are you doing here?" She didn't take his hand.

Brandon sensed the tension between the two, "Um XJ? He wanted to make sure you were alright. He set up this room and everything."

XJ folded her arms, glaring at him. "Well, thank you," she said; her voice strained.

"I know we haven't been close but I think of you as my niece. I'm here to help," the older man pleaded with her.

"Where were you when they took my momma away?" she said in an angry, low voice. "Why didn't the Revolution help her?"

He stiffened. "We warned your mother, but she wouldn't listen. She was stubborn."

XJ's body language said she wasn't convinced.

"Let's talk business." Brockman said, in his revolutionary leader tone.

"Oh, hell no! You aren't running me the way you ran my mother! This freaking Revolution ruined my family, but it won't ruin me! I'm not working with you—you wouldn't even help my mom!"

He sat back. "Your grandfather would be so disappointed in your behavior. He sacrificed himself for—"

XJ went totally Ebonics. "*Niggah*, don't tell me about my granddaddy's sacrifice! No one understands it better than me! I don't like your methods, and I *don't* trust you!"

Brockman cleared his throat. Brandon thought this brown haired, white man would freak when XJ called him the "N" word, but he stayed calm.

That's why I respect him. He's so much cooler than my dad. He almost wished Brockman was his dad.

The older man switched tactics. "Well, I see you're not a fan of the Revolution. Here, take my card. When you're ready, call me. I have some information that you might find important." He stood up and Brandon walked him out of the room.

"I don't know what's gotten into XJ," Brandon said. "I'll try to talk some sense into her!"

Brockman raised his hand to stop him. "No, son, she's decided not to trust us. I can't say I blame her. The Revolution has had to make some tough choices over the years, and they haven't always been in her best interest."

"But what will we do? We need guidance, leadership, support!"

The older man stared into Brandon's eyes. "Revolutions were built by young people. You have everything you need. Come to me when you want advice, but follow your own heart. CAGE will be overthrown by young energy—not by old revolutionaries." With that, he was gone.

Brandon walked back into the room. "Take me home!" XJ demanded. "I don't want anything from the Revolution!"

He felt shocked and hurt. He knew the Revolution could help, if she'd accept it. How could he convince her?

Chapter 24

"GEPs' freedom depends on independent revolutionaries telling their stories to the world, one by one."
—Brandon Miller, Revolutionary TV

XJ prepared to leave. Brandon put his arms around her. His lips caressed the back of her neck. God, she'd enjoyed him!

But her mind woke up. She put space between them. "As much as I enjoy our time. This is over." Her voice sounded final, but her body still responded to him.

He pulled her back against him. "I'm sorry. I just wanted to ... I just wanted to calm you down."

"I don't need to be calm." Her aggravated tone sounded stern even to her own ears. He stepped away, and XJ felt the chasm grow between them.

"Look," he said, "I don't claim to understand why you feel the way you do. But I respect Brockman. Sometimes I wish he were my dad."

"Don't say *that!* Don't say you respect that butt-hole! My grandfather and mother both trusted him and look where it got them." XJ's shoulders and neck tensed. "I just hate the Revolution and that crap they throw. It makes me so mad, I just want to implode; hold it, plant it in his brain, and explode inside his mind!" She threw her hands up in an explosive wave.

"But without their rhetoric, the Revolution would have died years ago."

"Look, if you're going to spout that mess, I'm definitely ready to go. Those revolutionaries are all about talk. But when it comes time, they're short on action. When things get bad, Brockman gets gone."

Brandon got up and sat next to her. "Well ... I want to help you as much as I can. CAGE killed my mother and I swear that I will do everything that I can to make sure they can't kill yours, too."

XJ stared at him. "I didn't know." Her voice was very small now.

Brandon continued, "I don't know what Brockman's story is, but I know mine. You can trust that I'll do whatever it takes to help you. If you let me use the power that I have to support you, I will. Just say the word."

She thought for a minute. She needed the help. She'd turned her back on Brockman and the Revolution, but Brandon? Should she turn her back on him?

"By your power, you mean your Internet TV show, don't you?" XJ asked.

"Yeah ... it's all I've got, but I'll be fair to you and your family."

"Fine." She winced. Maybe he could be helpful. "If I work with you—we can't, you know, be together."

XJ did not want to become her mother. Her mother's revolutionary boyfriends over the years drove a wedge between her mother and father. She didn't want to tell Brandon that Brockman had been one of Dorothy's lovers. He destroyed her parent's marriage. She would be stronger than that. It was too much and she wouldn't mix revolutionary business and puppy love for anyone.

He moved closer to her ear and spoke a soft whisper, "So you'll let me do the story but I can't hold or kiss or caress you?"

Hot fire ignited through XJ's body. She kept her resolve. "That's right. You lose focus when romance gets involved." She closed her eyes as she responded.

Brandon's voice sounded strained, "Agreed. Where do we start?"

She moved to a position of power at the table. "By cutting a deal. I want to be your exclusive only. You can't show my likeness or my story without my approval. If I tell you to stop taping—you stop.

I also want the message to be fair. But show me and my family in a positive light."

He chuckled. "Should I take notes?"

XJ glared at him. "I'm not freaking joking, Brandon. You want to work with me," she pointed to herself and then to him, "then you'd best do what I tell you."

Brandon sat back in thought. "I can handle that. Agreed. So where do we start your story?"

"First, I'll go to the restroom and clean myself up. Then you'll interview me. After that you'll help me find my long lost relatives."

She stood up and went to the bathroom to get ready. That was just about all she could tell him. She definitely wouldn't share about her holographic grandfather and his lab. But she could use his resources to help her find her family. This could work to her advantage.

XJ closed the door to the restroom and took a deep breath. So much had gone on that she didn't know how to put it all together. She stepped over to the mirror and took a long look. Her nerves were raw. She turned on the water and frowned in the mirror.

Emotions threatened to take over, but she gulped another strong, clearing breath. She sighed, washed her face, and dried it with one of the motel towels.

Part of her felt really sad, but the other part listened to the strength and conviction in Brandon's words. "This is Brandon Miller reporting for Revolution TV."

XJ smiled. He seemed confident; sure of himself. She stood back and folded her arms to hear more. "I'm here today with XJ Patterson, the granddaughter of Dr. Gary Leonard Kates, who has suffered a terrible ordeal at the hands of CAGE. She's volunteered to give Revolution TV the exclusive on her story. Stay tuned."

Brandon paused. She could tell that he was nervous, maybe worried, but she respected his mission. She'd cleaned herself up, so she looked as presentable as she could.

Almost on cue, XJ walked out.

When she looked at Brandon, his eyes ran over her body in a heated way that made her squirm ... pulled at her inside. Her stomach knotted. If things had been different, Brandon would be the one that she'd give her virginity to.

But she couldn't think like that. She still didn't trust him all the way. It still hurt that he chose her white step sister over her. She'd have to be cautious. Too much was at stake.

He'd set-up a small interview area with lights, portable green screen, interview chairs, and a camera. He beckoned for her to come over and sit down. Naughty thoughts snaked in her mind, but she dismissed them. It was time to tell her story and she didn't have time for foolishness.

XJ sat in the interview chair. The lights warmed her face. What would she tell people? She fidgeted with her hair and outfit.

"Ready?" Brandon asked.

She took a cleansing breath. "As I'll ever be."

Chapter 25

"Best laid plans go all to hell when GEPs are involved."
—Nadia Stillwater, Director of CAGE Regional Office

Heather rounded the corner in the CAGE corridor. She had her plan all worked out. It was perfect. She'd have Brandon all wrapped in a bow for her mother.

Then the other Heather knocked inside her mind. *We could turn this to our advantage and be rid of mother once and for all.*

The thoughts made her stop, and rub her temples. She couldn't remember if she said it in her head or out loud. "You're too much trouble. I won't listen."

She kept walking faster, but her breathing quickened.

Don't ignore me! I'm telling you. If we work together, we both can get what we need. We both can be free.

Heather bit her lip and said, "What? What is it?" Her hands started to shake and her stomach felt woozy.

Is it a deal? Will you work with me?

Heather stopped and put her back against the cool wall. Her head kept spinning. But the other Heather was right. This would never end. She wanted to be done with all of this. She wanted to be free.

Was it possible?

She heard herself say, "I'll do it. Just tell me what to do." Her body slid down the wall and she sat on her bottom with her legs outstretched. She let go of her tension, and her shoulders slumped. The other Heather affected her this way sometimes.

"What are you doing?" She heard her mother's voice. "Get up from there!"

Heather jumped up like a soldier and straightened her outfit. She'd changed back into her pink combat boots, turtleneck, and hot pink jeans.

"Sorry, mother. I was just resting." Heather stammered.

"Who were you talking, too?" Nadia moved closer.

"No one. I was just working out my plan." Heather felt the fear-filled sweat run down her back. She made no move to do anything about it.

"Come." Her mother beckoned a group of doctors. One stood out. "Dr. Robinson, did you complete the task that I asked you?"

Dr. Robinson pushed his glasses up. "Yes, it's ready, but it's still experimental."

Heather watched Nadia move closer to Dr. Robinson. "Will it work? I'm not concerned about the effects."

Dr. Robinson cleared his throat. "Well, there will be short-term side effects but there's no way of knowing long term effects."

"Use it!" Her mother sneered. "I need to remove the X factor from my plan."

Heather loosened up a bit. She was glad her mother had no idea about her plans. She turned to walk away.

"Just a second, dear. I understand you let XJ go?" Her mother's laser eyes made Heather nervous.

"Yes. Yes. It's all a part of my plan. I'm on my way now to assemble my tracking team." Heather tried to sound confident, but the other Heather kept knocking. She rubbed her temple.

"Come here, sweetie." Her mother raised her hand. Heather didn't want to touch her.

Heather found herself surrounded by her mother and the group of doctors. From behind, she felt a needle prick the back of her neck.

"*Ouch!*" She screamed. "Why'd you do that?"

Her mother said. "Thank you, Dr. Robinson," as she turned towards Heather, "Just assurances, dear ... I sense that you're conflicted. This will help."

Heather rubbed the injection site. "I'm not conflicted. Can I go on my mission now?"

Nadia smiled, her eyes flat and cruel. "By all means, keep me posted."

Heather stormed off down the hall. But as she reached the door, both of her minds went blank. She rubbed her temples, frowning. Something was overwhelming her senses.

Her hunter abilities were ramped up. It was like she could *feel* the location of anyone she imagined. But her mind was fixated on Brandon. She had no conflict about it. She *wanted* him. She *needed* him.

She needed to find him and she did. Her mind tunnel focused. Before she knew it, her team was assembled and they were out the door.

"Miss Stillwell, we're approaching the location of the target." The CAGE officer snapped her back to reality.

"The Patterson girl is inside, but not alone." The second officer confirmed over the radio.

Heather allowed the anger to boil. Saskia's warm touch soothed her anger and calmed her instantly. Heather shrugged it away.

"Don't do that!" Heather whined. *Why the hell is she touching me anyway?* She felt her eyes change to red.

She whipped out her cell phone. Time to check her theory. Would Brandon respond? Over the next 20 minutes, she texted him twice. He didn't answer.

Heather screamed, "What is he doing in that dirty motel, anyway?"

Saskia moved closer to her so that they were close, but not touching. Her voice was smooth ... sultry but calming. "Do you really care?"

Heather checked her phone again. Still no answer. Heather's mind tanked. She grabbed her head—now in complete sensory overload. She was raw with the need to be near Brandon. She *had* to have him. She jumped up and smashed her cell phone against the console, and then she whipped around to face Saskia.

"Of course, I care!" Saskia shrunk back, but Heather didn't care. No one was going to keep her away from Brandon! She wanted to rip the tramp's face off!

"*I'm pissed!*" Heather let her anger out in full force—she felt like an addict. She wanted Brandon bad. She wanted to touch him ... to have him ... to love him. Heather's body shook. She slumped down in the chair.

"I've got to have him!" She yelled and sobbed.

Saskia pushed Heather's hair while lightly caressing her face. She breathed deeply, the sensation threatening to calm her. A part of her loved it, when Saskia touched her. Her body reacted in a way that felt different but right.

Heather focused again. "I've learned a few things about men. Sas."

"Is that right?" Saskia said with dry humor.

But Heather didn't feel offended. "I've learned that men respond to being manipulated. They like a woman to control every move. They like to be under the woman's scrutiny. It makes them feel good. It makes them feel loved. It makes them feel secure."

The more she talked about Brandon, the more she felt her tension ease. "In fact," she went on, "Brandon will marry me because I won't give up on him. He knows that I love him. One day, I'll find peace in his arms because I didn't give up on our love."

"So you're saying that men like to be stalked?" Saskia sounded thoughtful but serious.

Heather felt the confusion take over again. Her friend's question hit something *hard*. She pounded her head with her fist. Her hands shook and she broke out in a sweat.

"Don't you understand? I love him!" Heather slumped back down into the seat. Saskia moved behind her as she rubbed her back and neck. Heather felt her cares melt away. The young woman's touch melted her defenses.

Heather closed her eyes as Saskia's voice whispered into her ear, "I wish someone would love me like that. I wish someone would stalk me and never let me go."

She wanted to fall into Saskia's voice. Her body perked up ... she felt something tugging inside low. Maybe she should find a room so Saskia could give her a short massage. The radio cracked in the background.

Heather's abilities perked up. *What the hell? What am I thinking?*

"Miss Stillwell. We have confirmed the location of the targets. The subjects appear to be kissing." The CAGE officer's voice crackled off.

Heather felt the meltdown happening. She leapt from her chair and pushed Saskia back. "Get your hands off me!"

The murderous rampage took her over as she bolted towards the door. "I did everything he asked me to do! I was perfect! I *made* myself perfect! Why does he choose her over me? How can I get rid of this tramp?"

Everything inside her went eerily, stark-raving focused. Her tracking abilities heightened. She channeled on XJ, picked up a stun gun and kicked the back of the van open. That slut was going down today!

Someone shot her from behind. She felt the dart pierce her neck. Her knees crumbled to the pavement. Someone caught her head. The last words she heard were, "our mission is to watch, not engage the target."

"Douche Bags." Heather murmured. She'd been drugged.

The last thing she remembered was Saskia's fear filled face.

"I'll be okay, Sas, the tranquilizer will only last a few minutes and I can get back to him...." Her response sounded slurred even to her.

Saskia's eyes rounded wide and she looked sad. "That's what I'm worried about, love."

Heather's body went rigid and then numb. They couldn't keep her from her Brandon for long.

Chapter 26

"I just want people to understand that my Mom is innocent. I want to use everything that I can to save her from Zone 6. I'm not a leader, I'm just a kid on a mission to save her mom."

—XJ Patterson, Interview #1 on Revolutionary TV

XJ couldn't believe how well the interview went with Brandon. He asked smart questions. Hopefully, she'd gain a following and people would help or rally towards her cause. Mostly, though, she hoped that her mother would be freed.

She'd been thinking a lot about her mom. She really missed her. And she couldn't let these setbacks stop her. She was determined to save Dorothy.

Brandon looked hot. His Mustang was cool. XJ felt special riding with him. She wanted to tell him everything, but she held back, because she still wasn't sure if she could trust him with all her secrets. He seemed to be honest. Would he still choose Heather over her?

She couldn't be sure.

He reached over and squeezed her hand. Being with him felt so right.

Her voice squeaked. "Thanks for a great interview. I appreciate it."

Brandon's smile warmed her. "No problem. I just want you to know that I'm here for you—if you need me."

He pulled the car into her driveway. She relaxed in the seat. It was good to be home. Brandon got out and opened the door for her.

God, I'm crushing hard! XJ thought, as she got out and stood next to the car. With Brandon standing so close to her, it was hard for her to think. She'd convinced him to bring her home and here they were in front of her house.

The sun was dropping and it cooled the heat of the Georgia day, while a relaxed breeze brushed the two of them. It felt like a heavy embrace was inevitable. XJ's butt rested on the passenger door of his Mustang, as she looked up into Brandon's blue eyes.

She would never tell him that his presence sent hot messages up and down her back side.

"Why should I leave you here alone, again?" He sounded worried about her.

XJ was breathless, but she played it off. *I want him in a way that I've never thought about with another guy.* Outloud she said, "I've been through so much. I just need to process all of this *alone* for a while."

Another light breeze blew and she could smell cologne mixed with his masculine scent. She felt anxiousness shift low between her legs. Brandon moved closer to her and began to touch her face. She closed her eyes and a warm sensation shot through her.

XJ wanted nothing more than to rest inside his comfort, but she had to get things under control. There was too much work to do. She pushed his hand away. She could tell that it irritated him.

"Fine." He said. "But, I'm coming in to check things out. And I'm coming back first thing in the morning."

OMG, I don't want him coming into the house! That was the *last* thing she wanted.

If he came inside, she wouldn't want him to leave. One thing could lead to another ... with her granddad watching.

She pushed him back with both hands, a little harder than she intended. "No! I don't want YOU checking things out! I can take care of myself."

She'd almost escaped, but it seemed like he was prepared for her shove. He pulled her more into his arms. Instantly, XJ melted between him and his Mustang. She looked up into his eyes, smelled his maleness, the warmth of his embrace, and the low anxiousness spread up her body.

She wanted nothing more than to claim his lips for her own.

"Brandon, let me go." It was a small whispered plea. "I—I just need to clear my head. I promise I'll...."

XJ was losing it. She didn't want to be like her mother. It was the boyfriends that ruined her parent's marriage. She wanted to be stronger—to be able to work with a guy without adding romance. Dororthy's romances had screwed up her life, and filled XJ's with a ton of revolutionary "uncles" over the years.

She shifted her arms, and the ring her mother gave her brushed against Brandon's pants leg. It was so much so fast. Emotions overwhelmed her and the tears started. She buried her face in Brandon's chest and sobbed.

"It's okay." His voice quietly soothed her. "I don't want to leave you like this." Tender kisses touched her forehead.

Between the sobs and her intense feelings for Brandon, XJ felt swept away. How was she going to do all of this? Could she save her mother? Could she reunite her family without sleeping with him?

His kisses moved towards her hands, as he caressed the rest of her. She moved her hands away from her face. The tightness and his sweet closeness sent her body into overdrive and her mouth found his.

XJ felt his Mustang at her back as she lifted her arms and opened her body to his full weight. Her mouth watered and the sensation of the kiss sent wild messages through her mind. She'd lost control and fell deep into Brandon's kiss.

The worst part was she didn't want to stop.

Chapter 27

"GEPs must help each other. It's a necessity, but not a law."
     —Dorothy Kates-Patterson

"Trouble for GEPs comes from saying 'yes' too soon and 'no' not soon enough."
     —Xavier Patterson

Brandon had never felt this way about a girl. XJ brought out feelings he didn't realize he had. He wanted to protect her ... care for her ... and love her all at the same time. He deepened his kiss. Even though he could tell she was inexperienced, he wanted her all the more.

She's the one. I can feel it.

The kiss made his manhood rise. He wanted to put her back into his car and take her somewhere nice for her first time. She smelled so good ... he loved running his fingers through her braided hair. She tasted like dark chocolate. His leg buzzed.

What was that? Some sort of insect? The phone buzzed again. XJ broke off the kiss. "Um, your phone's ringing." She looked like she'd snapped back to the coldness.

WTF! He didn't care about the phone. He reached for XJ, but she pulled away. The moment was ruined.

He cleared his throat and stepped back. He pulled out his phone. *Heather's calling again.*

"Hello?" His voice croaked.

"Well, you finally answered your phone! Remember our deal. I'll haul your little jungle bunny back here with quickness, if you don't give me what I want...," Heather said, her voice ice cold.

He mouthed to XJ, *I need to take this,* as he walked around to the other side of the car.

Brandon watched her move towards the house. He didn't want her to walk away. He didn't want her to be out of his sight.

"I'm sorta busy now," he said; talking low so XJ couldn't hear.

"I guess you're sexing XJ!" Heather shot back.

"What? She's not that kinda girl." Brandon said, allowing the anger to flow.

"Oh, and I am? You didn't have any problem doing me!" He could hear the venom in her voice.

He sucked in his breath."Is there a point to this conversation?"

"You made me a promise and I expect you to keep it!" she snapped. "Meet me at the *Tuxedo Shop* at *Discovery Hills Mall* in 20 minutes, so they can get your measurements. I want you to look good on my arm." She hung up.

"Crap!" he whispered. He shoved his phone into his pocket and raked his hands through his hair. He wanted to stay with XJ, but he'd made the deal.

If I don't cooperate with this crazy girl, I don't know what she might do.

He trotted up to her door and knocked. The door opened and he walked into the living room. The house was dark and silent.

"XJ?" He yelled.

"Back here! I'll be out in a minute."

Brandon sat down on the sofa. This place was a wreck. He should hire someone to come over and help her get things set back up. He had more than enough money to cover it.

"Do you need me to help you with anything?" He yelled again.

"No, I'm fine." Her voice sounded closer. "I just needed to take a few minutes alone."

She walked back into the room and Brandon stood. "Look, something's come up. I don't want to leave, but I have to. Will you be okay?" He moved towards her to pull her into his arms.

XJ put her hand up to block him. "No, I mean, yes. I'll be fine. This...." She motioned her finger between the two of them. "Has got to stop."

"I understand." He said. His body disagreed. "It feels complicated." He wanted to kiss this all away.

"If we're going to work together, we have to keep cool heads." She sounded rehearsed.

His phone buzzed again. He glanced at the text message from Heather. It read: *WTF? Where R U?*

"Looks like you really need to go." XJ looked concerned. "I'll be fine. My mother has plenty of rations, hiding places, and tactical plans to keep me comfortable. I'll see you in the morning."

"Are you sure? Let me bring you something tonight. Food?"

She ushered him towards the door and his phone buzzed again. "I'll be fine. See you in the morning."

And just like that he was down the porch, into his Mustang and on the way to see Heather when all he really wanted was to comfort XJ.

Chapter 28

"Sometimes we forget what's most important to us."
—Heather Stillwell

Heather felt numb and shaky as she waited for Brandon at the Tuxedo shop. She bit down on her lip. The tranquilizer's residual effects irritated her, but she kept moving. Most Zone 6 detainees never noticed the effects, because they were tortured with stronger versions that knocked them out.

I should scratch those pricks' eyeballs out! How dare they treat me like a detainee! I'm gonna find a way to make them pay.

Her phone sung. Was it Brandon? "This is Heather," she answered. "Only the most beautiful girl in the world." Her hands trembled uncontrollably. "Oh, mother...." *What does she want?*

Brandon was all she wanted. All she needed. An image floated across her mind. It seemed harmless, but it continued to grow. Heather scratched her head.

Something was distracting her. Was it someone's lips? They felt soft....

"You there?" Her mother sounded distant. "I heard you had a bit of a struggle while on mission."

Heather's throat felt swollen and dry. She needed water. *Water!* She mouthed and snapped her fingers at the Tuxedo salesman.

"Yes, I did." Heather laid on her sweet, princess charm between gulping water. "I was so afraid and now I'm sick."

The fakeness came naturally. Her hands trembled more, as the sweat poured down her spine but that's not what was bothering her. More images assaulted her now. She held her head back and tried to cool off her brain. It worked, a little.

"I want those men gassed!" She whined with passion, but her words sounded unstable.

"Oh, that sounds awful." Her mother sounded like she was talking to a two year old. Heather sensed somewhere inside that she hated her mother. But she squashed those feelings.

"We must do something. I don't want to tarnish their splendid records. Anyone who works for me must be stellar...." Nadia went on, "But a good torture session will be okay. I'll put them in the gas chamber with something non-lethal but sickening." Her mother sounded like she just needed a reason to torture somebody. Heather's situation was an excuse.

Heather didn't care, but it was hard to focus on the conversation. Inside her brain, there was so much interference and images of soft caresses, lips. A warm headache began to spread across her frontal lobe.

"Will you give them a mask?" Heather tried to sound interested, as she rested her head on the big chair. "They don't deserve one."

"I must show mercy. I'll make them take it off after ten minutes." Nadia sounded pleased with herself. "All in the name of training and punishment. I love it!"

Heather's mind crackled like a thunderstorm. The headache spread from her frontal lobe to her entire head. She tried to control it, but her stomach lurched and the images kept attacking her.

"Thank you, mother. You're the best." Heather couldn't stop the hate that came as soon as the words left her mouth.

"You're my only daughter. I wouldn't have it any other way." Her mother rattled on, but Heather didn't hear. Her brain flip-flopped as the images rushed past her like a freight train. She dropped the water bottle, and smashed the palm of her hand on her forehead to stop the pain.

"Heather, you there?"

Is she still talking? Heather sensed rage over something but couldn't remember what it was.

Just then, her Brandon walked into the store. Heather's abilities flared. She could sense that her eyes turned red. The hunter took control.

"Heather, you there?" Her mother's fake concern sickened her. Heather had to get rid of the old....

"Yes. I'm sorry, something's come up." Heather's singular purpose came into view. Brandon was all she needed.

"I just wanted to remind you, dear, to stay on mission. I need your help on this, okay?"

"Okay," *Whatever ... I just want this old bat off the phone!*

"Smooches!" Nadia hung up.

Heather smashed her phone together and all her attention focused on Brandon. Everything in her world popped into place. Her stomach stopped lurching, and the images subsided.

Finally, she could focus on her one true love.

Chapter 29

"Once a GEP has found his or her purpose, CAGE had better watch out!"

—Dorothy Kates-Patterson, Revolutionary Conference

XJ moped around after Brandon left. She actually missed him. She picked up items around the house and then slumped onto the couch.

She began to twirl the ring around her finger. Thank God that Brandon had completely rerouted all of CAGE's internal cameras into a continuous loop. They wouldn't be snooping around her anymore.

XJ had accepted that her situation was unusual, but she wasn't ready to call herself a revolutionary. Once she'd saved her mom she would simply put all of this behind her.

Suddenly something deep inside her, compelled her to get up and walk over to the lab's entrance. The door swooshed open.

Are those voices?

She marched into the heart of her Granddad's lab.

"Granddad ... who's here?"

XJ froze and then her smile grew. *"Dad, I've missed you!"* She ran over to her father and hugged him deep. *He did come to take care of everything!*

White dust swirled about the room.

"Hi, honey! I'm so glad to see you!" Xavier rubbed her hair back into place.

"Do you know what happened to Mom?"

"I do—I do. Gary and I were just discussing it." XJ could see her dad's distaste for her grandfather.

Her father's form shimmered. Was he holographic, too?

"Dad, what's going on?" She moved closer to him. He'd hugged her so he had to be real.

"It's my teleportation ability. I can't seem to hold it when my physical body is so far away. I'm still in South America." She could tell that the words hurt him.

"Oh...." XJ's face dropped. "So I'm alone after all."

Her father's form shimmered again, as he rubbed her chin. "I love you. I'll try to make it back to you as soon as I can."

XJ tried not to cry, but the tears spilled over and ran down her face. "How am I supposed to take care of all this! I'm just a kid!"

"I know, honey ... I know. Your grandfather and I have talked about this. I—I want you safe and away from here, but he wants you to fight." Xavier's voice cracked. She could tell he was concerned and mad at the same time.

Dr. Kates cleared his throat. "She comes from a long line of leaders. She's got to pick up the fight, Xavier! You know as well as I do that—!"

"She's a child, Gary! She's a baby. My baby." Xavier grabbed XJ and hugged her closer, but his body began to shake.

"Dorothy won't survive if she doesn't try!" Her grandfather sounded sure.

Her father began to shake harder and to sweat. He pulled back and forced his eyes to meet his daughter's. He was a full foot taller than her.

"XJ, I can set something up so you can be with me in South...." Her dad's legs crumbled and he screamed.

"Dad!" XJ yelled. "Dad, how can I help? Granddad *do* something!"

Gary looked sad. "You're the only one who can help your parents, doll. He needs Dorothy's ability to keep him together."

Xavier's long form shook and convulsed. XJ fell to her knees, and put his head in her lap. "What are you talking about? They haven't been together in years!"

Her dad smiled. "It's okay. I'll be fine. I just can't hold my form on this side. I'll come back. I promise...."

He disappeared. "Dad, *dad!* Where are you?" XJ screamed at the top of her lungs until they burned. She slumped down.

"Are you telling me that now I have to save *both* of my parents?" XJ shouted looking horrified.

"It would appear so." Gary sounded sad. "But you must save your mother, first."

"Look, Granddad, I'm not like Mom! I don't enjoy being a revolutionary! I don't want to be like her. I'm not interested in this for the long term."

She could see his face measuring her. "Doll, this isn't a path one likes. Your mother and I chose this because it's what we had to do."

"I—I know. It's just that Mom gets off on this. I can't be like that. I just want to be a normal girl. You know?"

"I know. I know." She could feel true emotions coming from a holographic image. *How freaky is this?*

She continued. "You were right. I can't save my mom using conventional methods. They just don't work. What's worse, I was tortured."

"Oh, XJ! I wish I could've taken this on for you! I wish I wasn't holographic." He seemed earnest, sincere.

"Well, what do I have to do? Mom's out there alone. CAGE is probably torturing her. I've got to do something to stop them from swiping her mind or killing her. How can I do this alone?"

Her Grandfather turned toward his wall of computers, and began working from the inside. The keys tapped like a piano that played alone.

"I've figured out a little more about your two cousins. But some of my memory is degraded. So there's a lot that I still don't know—like names—but I do have DNA signatures."

"You're saying Mom has other siblings out there, and you don't remember them?"

Dr. Kates hesitated and then nodded. "Exactly. I'm not sure why that is either. Dorothy probably knows or knew. But in order to protect us all, I believe I gave everyone a very specific mind swipe. You probably would've remembered your cousins, if I hadn't have done that."

XJ sat back. This piece of information slammed her in the gut. "So you mean to tell me that I had memories that were swiped away—of a real family, and cousins that could've been like sisters to me!"

Gary sighed. "Yes, it would appear so. I can only say I did it for everyone's protection. But now it's a huge inconvenience."

"No kidding!" XJ leaped from the floor, and began to pace. She wanted to smash something. That wouldn't help. "So tell me what you do have."

"Well, it appears I had images of all of you as children; as well as DNA samples."

"Had?"

He cleared his throat. "Well, I still have the clear DNA patterns but not the names and images. I have a name, Ector Rodriguez, or the Bibliotecario."

"What kinda name is that? The Biblio-te-cario?"

"He's the leader of a human information repository hive," Gary shot back quickly.

"What? So this dude is some sort of GEP librarian and has all of our information stored inside his hive?"

"I believe so." he continued. "It looks like your mother found his location, and set-up a time to extract the information brain-to-brain before her abduction."

"How am I going to convince this Biblio-dude, err, hive to give me the information now that mom is gone?"

"Well, he wasn't actually giving them to her, but to her alter identity, Joanne Chesimard, the social worker."

"This just keeps getting better and better!" XJ slapped a table. "My mom had a secret identity?"

"Yes." Her grandfather's holographic image looked concerned. "But I don't know all the particulars."

"Hold on a sec." XJ tore out of her grandfather's lab and into the house.

She remembered some of her mother's papers that had some dates and times. She almost fell apart inside her mom's room. It was so hard for her to keep it together. She found what she was looking for and bolted back to her grandfather. The lab doors slammed shut.

She spread out an agenda, paperwork, and sticky notes on the nearby table "I came across these when I was looking for something that might free mom."

"Indeed." Her grandfather touched his holographic forehead.

"I thought they were worthless, but now I'm thinking that these were actual dates that she made with this info Biblio-teca dude." XJ sat on the couch, and stretched her arms over her head.

Her grandfather studied the paper trail. "Yes. This looks like the appointment here. It's for tomorrow morning."

Her grandfather rubbed his beard while he studied. "I believe you're right, doll. Your mom was on her way to figuring out about your cousins before she was caught."

"What should I do granddad? Should I go?" XJ wished he were real and could do this for her.

"I can't answer that for you XJ," his face looked grave. "That's something you've got to decide for yourself. But if you don't find your cousins and reconnect with them, I can't see how you'll free your mom."

Was she ready to follow in her mother's revolutionary footsteps? Could she do this? She wanted to cry, to scream—to moan. This impossible situation called for an insufferable solution. It called for her to give up her idea of being normal. And become something that she despised.

"I'll have to do this granddad. Will you help me?" XJ's voice sounded insecure.

"I will, doll. I will."

The tears flowed slow at first and then picked up momentum. She wanted to be like other GEP teens, oblivious and living their lives. Instead she was stuck trying to stop CAGE from harming her mother, and taking over the world.

Her grandfather tried to soothe her as best as he could. But ultimately, she had to pull herself together. She needed a plan but what?

"Tell me about the Bibliotecario, and my mom's alter ego Joanne Chesimard."

Chapter 30

"It's hard to be somebody else."
—XJ Patterson

XJ needed Brandon's help to find out more about the Bibliotecario. Gary knew the function of a GEP with the information repository ability. But the particulars were missing.

She needed Brandon to hack into CAGE's files to find out any strengths or weaknesses that she could exploit. She texted him. *Dude, I thought you wanted in on this story?* He didn't answer.

She was worried. Did CAGE have him in custody? Her heart beat faster. *I have to put this behind me. One of Mom's first rules was to assume the worst and go on with the mission regardless.*

XJ pushed her worry aside and focused on the information that she did have: Joanne Chesimard. "OK, granddad. Now, how are you going to turn me into Joanne Chesimard?" She squirmed.

"Well, doll, it's a simple process of manipulating your DNA in order to simulate the facial structure of Joanne Chesimard. I helped your mother create a completely, different persona. So no one would suspect her for snooping."

"Sick, but cool!" XJ sat back in the chair. "Will this hurt?"

"You will feel some uneasiness ... I've had to make some adjustments since you obviously are missing some, well, fully mature female parts." Gary chuckled and cleared his throat.

"Granddad, are you laughing at me?" XJ laughed with him.

"Just making some observations." He studied his computer screen while his keyboard continued to type. After a few minutes, he went to a receptacle door and motioned to XJ to open it.

"Now, take out the hyperspray, and release the contents into your system. But I need you to lay down on the gurney, so I can use my metal hands, if needed."

XJ got everything and hopped up on the lab table. "How long with this last?"

"Slow down, doll. You have a million questions. You're going to feel a lot going on ... it shouldn't really hurt; just feel a little uncomfortable. But once you're done, the effects will last about two hours. This is just a trial run."

She relaxed and let the hyperspray release. The metal arms clicked. At first she didn't feel anything. Then, suddenly her breasts became sore and her behind swelled. She started having hot sweats and then she felt cold.

What was that? "Granddad are you sure this is okay? I feel hot and cold at the same time."

"It's the hormones. We're adding things that a forty year old woman would have, and hot flashes are treacherous."

"I don't like this!" XJ's body bowed and she shrieked. "My butt feels like oozing jelly!"

Her body's molecular structure broke down as XJ convulsed and shook. Her body filled with water and things ... began to push out. With a spinning head, she let out another squeal, as the hot flashes took her under.

Is this what mom felt? She never wanted to experience this again.

Her body stopped convulsing. Her head felt like someone had pimp punched her.

"Beautiful, *beautiful!*" Her grandfather sounded like a mad scientist. "Go look in the mirror."

The metal hands released and she rolled off the table onto unfamiliar legs. Her body felt weird. She found her image.

"Ah!" She yelled and shrieked, "Who *is* that?"

"Well, it's a much fatter version of your mother, with a few additional DNA enhancements. Since you and your mom have similar DNA structure, you can easily look like this version of her someday."

XJ twisted her body around in front of the mirror. "I look like one of my fat teachers at school! What's with this big butt?"

"We had to pick someone opposite of your mom physically so we just let nature free."

"You mean mom had to deal with this, and go back to herself?"

"Yup."

"God ... she deserved a medal for enduring. Anything to be a revolutionary." XJ continued to study her face in the mirror. "What next?"

"Now, we need to test out your disguise. You need to take a short trip." Gary wrung his holographic hands. "I need you to take a trip to the mall."

XJ awkwardly dressed and left the safety of the lab. Her body felt different but she pushed on. She left the house, and found the white government vehicle that her mother had stashed in the back.

It was right where her grandfather said it would be. She was certainly on her own and afraid. But she had to test out her new disguise, and what better way than at the mall?

She'd drop in and purchase a small briefcase as well as withdraw $500 from the ATM. Apparently her mother had been paying the information broker on a payment plan. Tomorrow would be the last payment.

Thank God Mom took such good notes ... and I was able to figure out what to do.

She backed out of the little shed and down the back driveway. She felt awkward driving in her new body. But, she didn't feel uncomfortable driving. Dorothy hadn't allowed XJ to get a real license because she'd thought CAGE would trace her. So she made XJ stay under the radar.

It was the story of her life. Her mother never sent her to driver's training like other teens, because she'd already learned to drive from the age of ten. XJ could drive any type, size, or shape vehicle—just in case she had to escape—but she would have loved to have a real license.

XJ headed for the mall. Her mind filled with thoughts of Brandon. She was surprised that he hadn't texted her back. Something must have happened and now she was really worried. He wouldn't have left her like this without trying to contact her. She sped up. The mall would be closing soon and she wanted to test her new face.

She mashed the accelerator.

Chapter 31

"Sometimes GEPs have to cut deals with the devil, in order to learn the truth."
—Dorothy Kates-Patterson

This is like the sixth tuxedo that I've tried on. Brandon didn't want to be bothered with Heather. He wanted to be rid of her.

He stomped off to the dressing room again and slammed the door. She was driving him to homicide.

"Brandon, don't be upset with me. I just want you to look good." Heather crooned outside the door.

He raked his hands through his hair. He actually liked this tux. He stood tall in the mirror and posed. He liked it better, if he were wearing it to take XJ to the pageant.

"Try this one. Heather slid another tux over the door. "You'll look sensational in it."

Brandon huffed, but took off the one he liked. When would this end? If he took forever maybe she would go away. He took his time. *God, I miss XJ.*

He heard Heather talking to the sales guy. "Yes. Isn't my boyfriend cute? I just love picking his outfits."

Another female voice said. "Well, aren't you lucky?"

Heather said, "Luck? I think not! He's my soul mate. We'll be together forever and ever and ever."

Brandon finished putting this tux on, and shoved the dressing room door open. "Can we hurry this up? I've got something to do."

He made a quick dash to the dressing stage before Heather could change her mind.

"Silly. What's more important than getting ready for me?" Heather sauntered over to him and adjusted the collar. She pulled his face down and tried to snuggle his nose. He turned his head and looked in the mirror. He hated this one. His shoulders slumped.

Heather cleared her throat. "Um ... I love this one. We'll take it."

Brandon felt the room spinning with the hands of salespeople and alterations. Out of the corner of his eye, he saw Heather beaming with joy. She kept rattling on about being soul mates and getting married. His mind wandered to XJ.

"Darling, don't you just love this one? It brings out your eyes and it'll match my dress."

Brandon grumbled.

"He's just a little sensitive," Heather continued. "He knows how important this is to me."

Was she batting her eyes? *Yuck! I can't wait to get out of here.* How could he get away from her?

This tux made him feel irritated and uncomfortable just like Heather. Finally, they finished the alterations. He could see that she was distracted. He moved quick.

He got his clothes off, gave the tux to the seamstress and was out the door in a flash. He heard her in the background telling the sales guy how they were meant to be together as he slid out the door. He'd done what the deal required but he wasn't hanging around to be verbally stalked.

He found himself wishing again that he could take XJ to the pageant. But with everything going on and Heather being able to make CAGE abduct XJ, it was better for him to humor Heather and keep XJ safe.

He'd just about made it to his car when he heard Heather's crazy, crooning voice behind him. "Brandon! Wait up, dear! Brandon!"

He'd thought he'd dodged the stalker's bullet for the day. He groaned but kept his fast-paced walk. He wanted to get back to XJ. He was worried about her staying alone all night. So he'd decided to park outside her house, and watch from his car. He was so engrossed in his thoughts, that he didn't notice that Heather had caught up to him.

Is she talking? She's like a giant tick.

"Brandon! Stop!" Heather's voice ground into his nerves. He shook her off.

His phone sung. He flipped it and saw the text from XJ. She had new information. Good. He'd zeroed in on his car.

"*Stop!* Or I'll make you suffer!" She sounded serious.

Brandon sighed deeply, and stopped. *How can I get rid of her?* He wondered if he could ignore her away. "What do you want Heather? I did what you asked," he said, not hiding his intense aggravation.

Heather snatched his phone. Before she flipped it, he used his technopathic abilities to block the screen; so she wouldn't be able to see.

"Who's calling you?" Heather stammered, mad.

Her hands are really, really shaking. Weird? Is she like on drugs? Brandon snatched his phone back. "Doesn't matter."

Heather looked like she wanted to bite him. "You will tell me. We're together and you will respect me."

Brandon chuckled. What was she talking about? This chick was insane but he'd play along for XJ's sake. "We have an arrangement that I'm honoring."

He saw the realization slide across her evil eyes. Her composure switched. She straightened her back, like a rattlesnake about to strike.

"You're right. We have an arrangement." He could tell there was more behind her words. His phone sung again. He flipped it open. It was Brockman. Brandon began to text back when he noticed Heather's glare.

She pointed her finger at his face with an evil grin. "You *have* been receiving my calls and texts. But you've been ignoring me."

Duh. Brandon thought. "I've done everything you asked." He said with casual detachment.

She cleared her throat and walked closer to him. This didn't feel right. He backed up.

"When I call or text you, you will respond immediately. Or things will get very ugly for you and your little jungle bunny."

Yadda Yadda. He'd heard her threats before. But something about her was different this time. She seemed ramped up on something. What was it? He decided to wait. Let her finish her rant.

"I'm thinking that I know something, Brandon." She started singing her words in a creeped up tune. "It seems that you need more incentive to make me a priority."

Brandon stood up straighter. *She's trying to punk me!*

Heather continued singing her question. "Wouldn't you like to know what I know about your mom?"

She twirled around him like an evil princess, but her question stung deep. What did she know? She had his attention. He stood stock still, as Heather pranced around and played with his hair.

"Do you know that I have access to all the information about you and your family?"

Brandon's stomach lurched. He pretended to be calm. "Tell me. What do you know about my mother's murder?"

He died inside by letting her manipulate him, but he needed to know. He'd tried so many times to hack CAGE's firewall but always came up empty.

Heather gave him her faux princess smile. "Will you do what I want? Will you be mine, again? Will you treat me the way you used to?"

Brandon hesitated. He had to know. But he didn't want to be any closer to her or cut any more deals. How long could he play with her? He could never treat her like he used to. His heart belonged to XJ now. But he needed the information about his mom. He needed to know to free his soul.

"If the information is worth it. Maybe...." He felt like he was making a deal with the devil's daughter.

Heather smiled and grabbed his hand. She danced him back inside the mall.

"Looks like we'll be having dinner."

Brandon ground his heels and stopped. "Oh no! You haven't given me anything to make me want to have dinner with you. I only have fake innuendos. How do I know that you know anything?"

Heather smiled again. This time she looked like a pink princess with snake fangs.

"You've been hacking the firewall for years—trying to get in and when you do—you can't find anything. CAGE knows what you can do. I read the file. I can get it for you, but only if you play REALLY nice with me."

She stood up on her toes and gave him a sickening smooch on the lips. "Play with me, Brandon. I have everything you need."

He dug his fingernails into his palms. He needed the information about his mom. But he knew that he was falling for XJ. Could he play with the pink princess long enough to get what he needed? Would this ruin his relationship with XJ? It was a chance that he'd have to take.

Resigned, he said, "Let's get dinner."

Chapter 32

"These experimental drugs are unstable, but have been shown to boost GEP abilities by leaps and bounds. I'm not sure, though, if there's burn out or burn up for the GEP."

—Dr. Winfred Robinson, CAGE Medical Team

Heather's hands trembled, while she and Brandon walked to the food court. She made a quick move and locked arms with him so he wouldn't notice. Now was not the time for her to come unglued. Finally, she had what she wanted. Touching him made her feel calm.

I have my target ... I mean my man, close.

Her body relaxed and the hunter receded. She felt normal. She smiled. The disturbing images subsided. Being near Brandon helped her mind to knit or bond. He adored her. He just needed an incentive to get him back on track.

God, he's gorgeous and he belongs to me. I wouldn't let that XJ steal his affection.

"I'd love it if we could eat at *Panini*. It's my favorite restaurant." Heather rubbed her wobbly hand down Brandon's back. She bit her bottom lip. She wanted to smack herself. How could she stop this shaking? Instead, she smiled wider and pushed her breasts out.

Would one of my white pills help? But, she couldn't take one in front of Brandon. She wanted a kiss.

Her eyes went red. In a fast move, she pulled his face towards hers and put a wet, sloppy kiss on his cheek. His cheek? That's not what she wanted. She could sense his anger. He'd turned his face.

"Stop playing. What do you know?" Brandon could be so rude. He knew he wanted her. He knew he needed her. Why was he pushing her off? The distance made it hard for her to get her thoughts right. She needed to touch him. But he held her hands back. Would he notice the shaking?

"Don't rush me." Heather fought back real tears. She needed him. Couldn't he see? Her world became unhinged. Her neck tensed. She wet her lips, but found it hard to keep her emotions under control. She had to keep him. She made a plan.

"I'll sit over there while you get me my favorite smoothie. You do remember what I like?" Heather tried to make her tone steady.

Had Brandon smiled? Heather knew he still loved her. He remembered.

"Can you have them add extra protein powder?" She said in a syrup voice.

Brandon was gone and her mind went wild. She needed to touch him. Her hunter-self could not be controlled. She sat back in the chair, trembling, sweating. Her hands were uncontrollable. She ransacked her purse and dug out her pills. She popped ten of them. She didn't need water.

Her body relaxed, a little. But it seemed like the pills only worked part of the time. Her abilities were growing so quickly. She felt like she was on the edge of burn-out. Memories streamed through her mind. Had someone given her a shot? She couldn't remember and then those sweet lips crashed back. She heard another voice inside her head, but it was faint, small, whisper.

"*Let me out.*" Heather leaned forward and grabbed her head.

She wanted to scream. She wanted to yell, but her honey was walking up. Her abilities subsided. She needed to touch him. He was so sexy. Heather loved the way he walked. Her toes curled. She felt overjoyed. She'd won him back. He did want her. He did love her. He did care about her.

She couldn't control the excitement in her voice, "Thank you, lover." She lifted up so he could give her a kiss on the cheek.

"Here." Brandon shoved the cup in her face. He seemed to have forgotten her little kiss. He'd remember soon.

"What do you know, Heather? I'm on a schedule." Was he irritated with her? She couldn't believe it. He had to love her.

"What?" Heather's mind was still fuzzy. She hoped her pills would kick in.

"Stop screwing with me! What do you know about my mom's murder?" Brandon seemed to be gritting his teeth. Heather couldn't understand why he seemed so angry. This used to be their favorite spot. They'd had so much fun here. He was making this date uncomfortable.

"Calm down, lover." Heather took the time to relish her smoothie and look deep into Brandon's eyes.

His voice was an angry, pleading whisper, "Heather, what do you know?"

"Gosh. I know a lot." Heather continued with a lover's banter. "But I won't tell you unless you agree to my conditions."

She watched Brandon plop down into the nearest seat, sit back and fold his arms. "What do you want?"

That was more like it. She had his undivided attention. She loved how he focused on her. She loved how he made her the center of his universe. She loved how he gave her the attention she deserved.

She straightened her back to lift up her breasts higher. She knew how much he loved them. Then she swung her hair back and gave him a pose that would bring him to his knees with undying love. It felt so good to be confident and together.

"If you want my information, you'll have to be my boyfriend again." She said in the happiest, most loving tone she'd ever had. Her heart pumped with excitement. She'd get her man back and everything would be wonderful again. She'd be back at the top of the food chain. Her abilities snapped inside her mind.

Here it comes! She thought. *He's mine again!*

Brandon leaned closer to her and looked into her eyes. Did she see love?

"Let me think about it." She watched Brandon scrape and scoot his chair back then walk away. He did it so fast, she didn't have time to say something back. He'd be back. No way he didn't love her. He'd be back begging for what she had. She knew it. But what if he didn't come back? She had to convince him.

Her mind tumbled. The further he walked away, the less she could control her hunter abilities. He couldn't get away. He was her anchor. Heather leapt up from her seat and chased him down. He had to be hers and that was all to it. She had something that would make him belong to her.

"Brandon!" She yelled. She'd do anything to make him love her. *Anything*.

Chapter 33

"Do you really want to know what's hidden?"
—John Brockman

Brandon stormed down the walkway. He felt conflicted, angry, upset. Did Heather really have any information about his mother's murder or was she just playing him? He heard her voice screech behind him, but he kept walking faster. The wound from his mother's death struck him hard.

Heather playing me like this just pisses me off!

She caught him as he was headed out the back corridor. It was just him and her in the secluded hallway. He should keep walking. But what if she knew something for real? He'd been hacking into CAGE for two years trying to find something. Was what she knew worth it? He tried to keep cool.

"I know you'll want what I have." Heather said breathless. "I'll give you a little and share more with you but only if you'll agree to be mine."

Is she pushing up on me again? Brandon couldn't stand her. He clenched his jaw. He was sick of her manipulation.

He looked her up and down. "You don't have anything. If you did, then you'd have already used it." He pushed away and continued his marathon walk down the corridor.

"Wait!" She grabbed his sleeve and held him back. "I can prove it." She pulled out her cell phone and scrolled down to the document.

"I won't insult you with something minor. But I won't give you everything until you agree to be my boyfriend again." Her voice was breathless.

"Use your ability to tap into my phone, and check the authenticity of this memo." Heather was trying really hard to convince him. He hesitated.

I should walk away.

Instead, he closed his eyes and hacked into her phone. He raided everything that he could and stored it in his memory. He found the document. It said:

Memorandum

To: XXX

From: CAGE Cleaner Patrol

RE: Control Todd Miller by using deadly force against his mate.

It has come to our attention, that Mr. Miller has repeatedly refused to comply with our direct order to add subliminal messages to GEP Network, to enhance our control over the GEP population. We've tried many tactics to encourage him to comply. All have failed. He must understand the seriousness of his decision not to comply. Herein are your orders. Create a special task force to eradicate his mate. And leave a calling card that his offspring will be next, if he continues further resistance. Make sure that this is done in secrecy, and cannot be traced back to CAGE.

Brandon's whole body lurched. He felt sick. The memory of his mother's murder overtook him. He saw everything clearly. To think that she was murdered because of that stupid GEP network!

He was conflicted too. His dad had taken a stand and look what it cost him. He had to know more. Who had the cleaner patrol sent this to? He had to expose CAGE for what it was. He needed the rest of the information from Heather.

He gave Heather her phone and looked deep into her eyes. "Are there more like this?"

Heather smiled and rubbed his arm. "Oh, yes. There's a whole paper trail. But I won't give it to you unless you become mine."

He had to have that information, but he felt something deep with XJ and he wanted to help XJ save her mom.

Can I do both? He thought. "I need the information sooner. If you can give me more within the next couple of days. I'll be your boyfriend."

He could see joy ripple through Heather. What had he just done? Would he still be able to help XJ?

"Oh, I have more, boyfriend. I won't give it to you until I'm ready. But first, give me a kiss like you mean it."

Brandon narrowed his eyes and his body shifted. He felt the revulsion. He didn't want Heather. He didn't love Heather. He didn't care for Heather. She had what he needed, so he bent down and envisioned XJ's face. He kissed her as if his life depended on it.

He wondered how he'd be able to get out of this and get back to the love of his life. How would he explain this to XJ?

Chapter 34

"Things are not always as they seem but with GEPs you might see something that's unreal and believe it."
—Xavier Patterson

XJ skidded into the parking lot. She found a spot and pulled in easy. She loved to drive. She pulled the rear view mirror down and poked her new face. The flesh looked real enough.

Grandfather does good work. This would fool anyone.

XJ pushed her new body out of the car. Her breath rasped. She couldn't seem to catch it. *This extra weight is insane.*

She couldn't wait until the effects wore off. Huffing and puffing, she made it inside the mall. The air conditioner hit her face and the coolness soothed her.

Inside the mall, XJ felt odd. Her body was filled with new sensations. Awkward. Uncomfortable. Bloated ... and other feelings passed though her. She swallowed and gulped a huge breath. She could do this. But she had to get rid of the idea that she was a 17 year old, trapped in the body of a 40 year old woman—if she wanted to fool anyone.

As she rounded the corner, she bumped into a white couple by the movie theater. "Sorry, I didn't mean to bump...." The words caught in XJ's throat. *It was Brandon and Heather!*

Brandon spoke to her. "I'm so sorry. I didn't mean to bump into you, ma'am."

She leaned back with a dumb expression. The words stuck, but came, finally, "Brandon? Brandon Miller?"

Her voice sounded odd to her. It was deeper, different.

Brandon looked at her strange. "Yes, ma'am. Aren't you the social worker at my high school? Um, Mrs. Chesimard?"

XJ composed herself. She realized that she was in disguise. She'd have to play this game, but she was mad.

"Yes. Yes. I am." She gave a fake smile. She really wanted to punch him or cry. How could he do this to her? Her neck tensed and her lips trembled. She clenched her fists as she watched Brandon holding Heather with care. He seemed content, but she could see his discomfort. Maybe it was because he'd just bumped into an adult.

"Is this your girlfriend?" She held her fake composure.

Heather smiled at her with the happiest, most content grin. "Yes, he is, Mrs. Chesimard. We're the same mate-designation type, and we're going to get married someday soon."

Oh, how she hated her step sister! XJ's heart pumped fast. The betrayal hit her head. Had Brandon been playing her this whole time? She thought back to that summer wedding with the three of them. How Brandon chose Heather over her. The pain of it still stung. The mate-designation type all over again. She hated it.

She wanted to scream but she folded her arms together as she watched Heather give Brandon a kiss on the neck.

Her stomach turned over. Disgusted, she watched Brandon stand there mute with a stupid half-smile on his face. What was he playing? She wanted to use her telekinetic abilities on them both. Maybe she could throw them across the mall like rag-dolls.

She'd been a fool.

"Well, Brandon, you certainly get around. I thought I saw you with the little Patterson girl. What's her name, XJ?" She couldn't believe how smooth the words came out. She was certainly getting better at this undercover stuff.

Brandon turned red. Heather said, "Oh, no. He broke up with her. He's with me now." XJ watched Heather stroke Brandon's arm and plant a kiss on his left cheek.

"Isn't she your sister?" She wanted to punch Heather in the mouth.

"Oh, yes, ma'am, by marriage of course. My mother married her father. But we aren't close, like you'd imagine."

XJ felt the saliva build in her mouth. The anger pooled. She narrowed her eyes. *What kind of game is Brandon playing? He looks like a deer caught in the headlights. But then he didn't stop Heather from saying those things either. He just has this stupid look on his face—like he's a puppet or something.*

"Brandon are you alright?" She showed motherly concern; but she really wanted to smack him.

"Um..., yes. Yes, ma'am. I just. Well, XJ is just a really good friend that's all. She's been through a lot and I...."

"Oh, dear. You always take hardship cases," Heather simpered. "You're such a bleeding heart. That's why I love you. My sister is just his latest project. She obviously needs help with her mother being a criminal," she finished in a matter of fact voice.

"Is that true, Brandon?" XJ fumed.

He looked like he was going to combust. "Well, I.... Could you check on XJ for me? My family ... I mean my dad, er, Todd Miller, would really appreciate it."

Did he just use his dad's name? Brandon was trying to manipulate the social worker because his father was the school's benefactor! *He's acting like the rich brat that he is. He has a blond girlfriend, a rich father, and now his little pet social work project ... me.*

XJ's hair bristled on the back of her neck. *Smacking is in order, for sure, but I'm gonna chill.* "Well, I'll do that. So nice of you to take social work cases. You all carry on." XJ smiled a really fake big smile as she watched Brandon and Heather stroll towards the exit.

Their image was picturesque against the evening sky through the mall doors. The perfect couple held hands and smooched. She slumped her shoulders and almost broke down in tears.

It looked like she was on her own with a fresh broken heart.

Chapter 35

"GEPs play lots of games, but when they lose it's bad."
—Anonymous

Brandon finally escaped from Heather. She was like a smothering snake and he was glad to be away from her.

What a freak! It was late, but he had to see XJ. What would he tell her?

Truth be told, he'd begun to have very deep feelings for her. Just being with Heather proved to him that his heart couldn't hide. Inside, he was riddled with guilt although he was sure XJ would understand. Should he tell her?

If he could just hang out with XJ tonight, he knew that being in her presence would help calm him down so he could think. His Mustang tires crunched up the gravel to her driveway. He'd really missed her.

He wanted to know how her day went, and tell her why he couldn't text. He wanted to help her in the morning even if he had to skip school. He'd had such a day with horrible Heather. But he could spend his night with the love of his life.

He put his car in park and sat still. Finally, he raked his hands through his hair and took a deep breath. He hadn't decided yet how to tell XJ about Heather or if he should tell her at all. It might be better just to keep it to himself until he got the information. XJ would never know; and it wasn't cheating, after all.

He and XJ weren't really dating, yet. He'd have to fix that as soon as he got what he needed from Heather. Then, he'd make her his girl.

The night sky was pitch black, as Brandon walked up to the door. He knocked once, but didn't hear any movement. He rammed his hands deep into his pants pocket and danced from one leg to the other. He needed to see her bad. He hoped she wasn't sleeping or mad about him not texting back.

He knocked again and the door swung open. She looked so beautiful! He just wanted to hold her.

"What do you want Brandon Miller?"

"You're mad at me. I can explain." Brandon knew he should've tried to text her back.

XJ folded her arms. She looked really pissed. "I never want to see you again." She began to close the door, but he put his foot in the way as a brace.

He'd beg if he had too. "I'm sorry. I was just wrapped up today. I have another case that I'm working on...."

She looked at him with contempt. "Another case? Are you freaking kidding me?"

It all started to come out his mouth awkward and weird. "I just had to do this thing," he stammered. "I mean, this thing—it's not more important than you—but someone has information that I've got to have for my next story and I've got to...."

Before Brandon knew it, XJ was hysterical. Her eyes turned gray and her mouth twisted. He tried to grab her to calm her down, but she jumped back from his reach. Before he knew it, she reached back and slapped his face hard.

Boy, he thought, *this girl has a canon for a hand!*

"You are such a LIAR!" She'd used her whole body to push him out the door; and then she slammed it in his face. It locked before he could respond.

What just happened? Brandon rubbed his tingly face. Was she really that angry with him over not texting?

He needed to explain—to plead with her. He assaulted the door with knocks. "XJ. Please! Open the door! I can explain why I didn't text you back! I need to talk to you!"

The house went dark. There were no lights. No movement. No *anything*. He so needed to talk to her. Brandon sat down on the porch and opened his mind.

He used his ability to drop into her house's network. Since CAGE had cameras stationed around the house, he'd be able to locate her and knock on the window. She had to talk to him. He searched the whole house.

It was like she'd vanished.

He felt like crying. With learning the information about his mom's murder, forced to be Heather's boyfriend and now the loss of his true love; Brandon was on the verge of homicide. He jiggled the keys in his pocket and ran to his car. He needed to clear his head.

Chapter 36

"We all become something even if it hurts."
—Dorothy Kates-Patterson

XJ had a bad "all night" crying hangover. She rolled over and crawled out of her makeshift bed in her grandfather's lab. Her throat tightened, and she put her hands on the edge of the cot to steady herself. She stood up, slumped and tried to shake off the stiffness in her body.

She sighed, hanging her head low to stretch it as she stared at a spot on the floor. She took uneven breaths. Her yoga moves helped but the depression remained. How had all of this happened?

I need to get my mind right. She stood tall, grabbed her braids up into a makeshift pony tail, and walked on shaky legs to find some rations.

Her mother was good at making sure food was stashed everywhere. She found a brown package and ripped it open with her teeth. This was an MRE or Meal Ready to Eat.

I always loved the dehydrated breakfast—not! The MRE felt like a brick in her stomach—just like Brandon. *How could he do this to me?*

She couldn't afford to be weak. She guzzled a bottle of water and fixed herself so she was combat-ready. She brushed her teeth and washed up quick. Her meeting was in an hour, so she screamed for her granddad to materialize.

"Okay, doll, I'm here." A holographic Dr. Kates appeared, looking concerned. "What's going on?" His eyes were like lasers.

XJ did not want to talk about it. "I'm fine." She folded her arms tight. "Let's just get on with it. I picked up everything you needed."

Her grandfather smiled. "XJ, your mind has got to be right when on a mission. Or you'll get sloppy."

"I know this." She slapped her hands to her sides. "I don't need a lecture. I'm fine."

She let the anger rolled off in waves. Her heart raced, but she had to do this. Her mother and father needed her.

Dr. Kates sighed. He started talking about being careful and such. XJ tuned him out. Finally, he got to work. She lay on the gurney ... and in a short time, she was Joanne Chesimard, the 40-year old social worker again.

She stood up and allowed the sensation of the new body to hit her. This time she was able to handle the transformation better, even though it was still weird. Her heart ached. She ignored it. She dressed and was out the door after her grandfather had given her all his advice about the dangers of Information Retrieval GEPs.

They didn't seem all that dangerous to her. They were the GEP librarians and everybody knew that librarians weren't a threat.

She hopped in the car and cranked it up. She skidded out the driveway and raced down Rockbridge Road. It took her seven minutes to get to the *Extended Stay Motel* on Memorial Drive. Her mouth was dry and her lips tensed. She thought about Brandon and how she missed his support.

But she couldn't trust him. He'd never know her secrets. She'd cried and dried out.

Focus. She heard her mother's voice whisper inside her head.

She whipped the car into the parking lot and pulled into a spot. XJ swallowed deep and wet her lips with her tongue. She pulled the rear view mirror down and looked at herself.

You can do this. You must do this. You will do this.

She got herself together and looked up at the four-story motel. Apparently, Information GEPs co-existed in one location like a beehive. They needed to be in close proximity to one another. She pushed her door open and got out.

The residents peered over the side. Their stares were creepy. When she looked back, some retreated in fear. What was that all about? She took a deep breath and grabbed her briefcase.

Here goes nothing. She didn't like doing this but she wanted to save her mom.

A husky, Latina voice echoed from the motel, "Good Morning Miss Chesimard. Here to take our niños so early?"

XJ heard the sounds of an infant crying and a mother trying to calm the child so as not to draw attention. Her gut lurched.

She rubbed her nose. *What's that smell?*

XJ stopped and watched the yellow bus come for the elementary kids. The little GEPs hopped on the bus one-by-one. She slumped her shoulders and felt sad for them. They had to live in a place like this.

As her heels clicked, she heard a whispered gasp. "Not again! What does she want this time?" Hushes came out in a rush.

"Is she going to take our children to Zone 6, again?"

Had her mother done that? Would her mother have harmed innocent children? XJ allowed the knot to crawl up her spine. She was horrified but she couldn't come undone. She held her head up high. Thank God she had on a Navy blue suit so they couldn't see the sweat running down her back.

Her heels clicked on the motel catwalk. She had to find room 3b. Great, it was on the third floor. As she clicked up the stairs, doors slammed and people hid in fear. The stench continued to grow. She wanted to throw up.

"Is this the last time?" She heard another whispered voice. Her mind felt heavy, woozy.

"Tell Ector to give the cow what she wants! So she'll stop torturing our mind cell!"

What had her mother done? XJ felt a lump in her stomach. The stint up the stairs made her stop and catch her breath. But the long walk down to 3b made her jumpy and nervous. She kept looking behind her. These people were afraid of her. And people in fear did dangerous things.

She wished Brandon were here to watch her back. But she had to face this alone.

Chapter 37

"Certain drugs help GEPs improve their abilities, but they also give a false sense of confidence."
—Dr. Winfred Robinson, CAGE Medical Team

Heather walked through the school doors with her head held high. She'd put on her hot pink, power heels. She was back on top, confident, and empowered. Brandon was her man, again. She was right inside and everybody would see she was on her game. Best of all, she'd received a special shot from Dr. Robinson. She felt good.

"Hey, Heather!" Different students were jockeying her, but she ignored them. She didn't have to speak. They were beneath her. She sauntered over to her group.

Raven spoke first. "Hey, you look good today." Her other friends just stared. She knew they were in awe.

Heather swung her hair back and looked at Raven like she was under her shoe. "Brandon and I are back together, again. He loves me." Heather allowed her new-found confidence to puff up her chest.

Raven smiled a fake smile, and yawned. "Sounds good, I guess."

Heather didn't like her tone. The other girls moved back. *She's just jealous!*

Heather dug her nails into her palms, as the waves of fury crashed into her calmness. *Why are there always so many haters?*

"Well, we got back together and we had a great time yesterday. He treats me good." Heather moved closer to Raven and stood taller.

Raven snickered, showing her dimples. "Are you that foolish?" The other girls backed away, gawking.

Heather took a deep breath, but the anger railed. It wanted to be let free. She could feel it stinging inside.

"What the hell is funny?" Heather moved closer to her face. "Brandon is taking me—*me*—to the Miss GEP High School Pageant as my boyfriend! He's going to marry me! I'm on my way to being one of the richest GEPs in the world!" She squared her shoulders with her jaw set.

"Okay. If that's what makes you happy. Cool." Raven backed up and turned around to walk away. Heather's vision turned red and she zeroed on the back of Raven's outfit.

She thinks she's so cute in her hooker gray pumps, short skanky black skirt, and nerdy suspenders.

Heather let out an angry breath. Her hands shook, then her mind became unglued. Voices railed inside. She rubbed her temples and a headache blossomed. She wanted to scream, but people were looking at her so she chilled.

Raven should be happy for her. Raven always hated her. Heather grabbed Raven's shoulder and whipped her around. The girl's heels swooshed, clicked and slid on the tile floor. Raven had really made her mad.

What an ungrateful...! "You're jealous because you want Brandon for yourself. He's the best looking guy in school." Heather pointed a pink manicured fake nail at Raven's chest.

Another small group of students stopped and stared. They'd begun to build an audience. Heather's abilities took over. The headache spread, but she exercised control. She wanted to slap Raven, *hard*.

The young woman shrugged."If you say so ... I've got to get to class." She backed away like Heather was a rabid dog or something.

Tramp! The voices swirled inside her head, a heavy whisper. The extra noise inside her mind made her irritated.

"Stop!" Heather yelled.

Raven froze. Heather wasn't talking to her or was she? Since she'd stopped, Heather sized Raven up. The hatred spread. She thought she was cute with her sassy bob cut, dark hair and skinny figure. It was time to put her in her place.

Heather's voice got louder. "I can't believe how jealous you are! Brandon loves me and you want him for yourself." Heather allowed the hatred to radiate throughout her body.

Raven's dark eyes turned coal black then flickered. Heather couldn't move as those eyes pierced her soul. Heather sensed the girl's ability slither deep.

Raven hesitated, looked a little uncomfortable. She said in a spiritually calm way, "I'm not interested in Brandon. I just think you're wasting your time. He doesn't love or care about you."

Heather warmed inside as Raven's calm smothered her anger. She felt trapped. Everyone could hear this!

The small crowd instigated as they gawked, giggled. "Ooh, she's *doing* her."

How could Raven do her like this? Heather's hands began to shake. Her mind clouded. Her hunter abilities sprung to life. She wanted to scratch Raven's face, pull her hair, and smack her down.

"You've always wanted Brandon." Heather's voice sounded even, restrained and enraged.

Raven's coal black eyes gazed deeper into Heather's soul. She felt a trickle inside that made her woozy. She wouldn't fall for that, not again.

Raven's face turned vampire pale. She looked as if she were giving a premonition. "Saskia is your soul mate, not Brandon."

Heather lost it. "I don't like girls!"

She barreled into Raven and tried to dig her way to China through Raven's face. How dare she not be happy for her and

Brandon! Heather straddled Raven as she choked her and gazed into her coal black eyes. Was that fear?

Heather didn't care, she just wanted the slut to be quiet. Heather continued to choke Raven, but it wasn't working. Raven was still snaking inside her mind. She gave Heather a creepy smile.

Heather's hunter abilities went wild. This skank would stop laughing at her! They all would stop laughing at her!

She really thought she was cute with her perfect super model face. Didn't she know that blondes were better? Heather forced Raven to turn those eyes away by clawing her pretty face. No one would think she was pretty again.

Raven screamed and bucked underneath, but Heather had her pinned. "Shut your *mouth!*"

Heather's entire existence turned red. She grabbed Raven's skinny shoulders and lifted her up and down. Heather bashed and banged Raven's head on the tiled floor several times. It felt good to let it all out on Raven. Heather's mind calmed with every bang of Raven's head on the floor. Now, that stupid smile was gone. That tramp wouldn't cross her again.

Someone pulled Heather from behind.

"No! *No!*" Heather screamed. " Let me hit her! *Let me hit her!*" Heather lunged forward to try to stomp Raven's still form on the floor, but steel arms stopped her. She shrieked into the large chest that held her back.

"I demand you release me! Do you know who my mother is?" Heather shrieked, pleaded. She wanted to finish Raven off. She would show them all! Nobody would keep her away from Brandon. Nobody.

Heather swatted away something that pricked her neck.

"Douche bags!" She said in a drowsy haze ... and she went down, quick.

Heather woke up in an office. She groggily gazed at awards, trophies and certificates. Was she in the Principal's office?

I hate that prick.... What's his name? Mr. Branch. She got up off the couch and staggered to his chair.

Her head spun, but that was alright. She still felt really, really good. Her confidence was high. She plopped down in the Principal's chair and twirled around. Mr. Branch wasn't going to do a thing to her, but he had to pretend to everyone that she'd gotten in trouble.

She hated Mr. Branch. *He's such a wormy little weasel of a man.*

Heather's ears perked up. Her hunter abilities were growing. It was like supersonic sound. She could hear Branch talking about her.

His voice droned. "Yes. Ms. Stillwell ... I understand but we mustn't allow Heather's ability to manage her sensibilities."

OMG—he gets on my nerves! He's standing in the way of me and Brandon!

Heather's hands shook and the sweat poured down her back. She looked down at her trembling hands. Her pretty, pink fingernails were broken. She could still see traces of Raven's blood.

Serves that tramp right for not being happy for me and Brandon.

A small whisper inside her mind asked, *What have you done?* Heather ignored it. That voice wasn't in control. She was.

Mr. Branch kept going on and on. "Yes.... She's severely injured a student. We had to rush the young lady to the hospital. She may need reconstructive surgery."

Heather twirled and listened. *Circle, twirl, circle, twirl....* She swung and stopped at a mirror image. Her face was pallid, sallow. Her eyes had huge bags, and her blond hair was wild, unkempt. Heather screamed, loud, and then louder.

Who was that hideous beast? She looked like a monster or druggie. Her entire body shook as she tried to make herself presentable.

She looked at her pretty, hot pink outfit stained with Raven's blood. *Oh my God...!*

She couldn't get herself together. What was happening to her? She scanned the room, to see if she could at least find her hot pink purse and book bag.

I can't find it! Was her stuff still in the hallway? She had to stop the trembling.

Another voice snaked inside her mind. It didn't matter. She and Brandon were together. Her mission was accomplished. He would love her and only her now. She scratched her head.

Another voice told her that none of this was right. She really didn't like Brandon all that much. Her stomach churned. She placed her elbows on her knees and hunched over to drag her hands through the rat's nest that was her hair. She screamed, again and again.

She could still hear Mr. Prick droning on. "We would usually escort a student like this to CAGE's juvenile detention in handcuffs. But since it's your daughter, I thought I'd give you a courtesy call. Will someone from your office be here to pick her up?"

Mr. Branch cracked the door open while he held the phone. His tone was somber and still. He talked to her like she was a mental patient. "Heather, are you alright?"

He didn't care about her. Heather had had enough of him. She yelled, "Mr. Branch, you are such a freaking *idiot!* Just let me outta here so I can find Brandon!" Heather breathed deep but it didn't help. "I need my shot! I need my medicine!"

She leaped across the desk to strangle Mr. Branch. She saw terror in the man's eyes. He'd slammed the door closed, *quick,* before she reached him. Her soul ached. She didn't want people to fear her like this. Confusion and conflict filled her. What was wrong with her? She collapsed on Mr. Branch's desk in tears.

Heather heard him on the phone again, "Sorry, but your daughter seemed to have had a meltdown. Someone needs to retrieve and extract immediately."

She heard the phone hang up and shortly after the door clicked and locked.

She rolled around and shook uncontrollably on his desk. She cried. She yelled. She moaned. *Why am I like this? When can I get another shot? What about a pill?*

When can I see Brandon again?

Chapter 38

"At some future point, Information GEPs will be able to store millions of bits in one hive. But without the hive leader, there's no access. Bummer."

—Concerned Citizen

XJ found the room she was supposed to enter. Sweat rolled down her spine. It felt like insects were swarming around her—like she'd kicked a beehive. Is this what her grandfather warned her about? Information Retrieval GEPs lived together in a hive-like mind pattern.

Al Bibliotecario was a conduit or hive leader. He could extract the information and store where the others only held information in the recesses of their minds, but couldn't retrieve it without him.

She raised her shaky hand to knock on the door. Did she feel someone looking at her or was it her imagination? Could they really see through each other's minds? A baby cried and she heard a mother consoling it. She knocked on the door again and it creaked open.

She took a deep breath. *Here's goes nothing.*

XJ entered the darkened room. It took her new eyes a few minutes to adjust. The door slammed behind her. Her mind clouded with a million buzzing bees. She calmed herself and erected walls. *That's what granddad told me to be mindful of.* The hive-like mind would try to suck her in—she had to be open enough to receive the information. But not so much that they could use her like a puppet. Her breath shuddered.

A squat of a man walked out. He was five foot one, but walked with the attitude of a dictator.

She heard her new voice say, "Ector, so good to see you again."

The buzzing inside her head worsened. She controlled her fear. When she concentrated, it felt like walking through honey.

Al Bibliotecario smiled. He spoke in a singsong broken version of Spanish and English, "Ms. Chesimard.... So good to see you."

He walked closer. *OMG...! What is that smell?* He reeked. Her granddad didn't say anything about that. His odor was a rank body odor, mixed with a metallic version of Old Spice. The stench linked to his power-base. XJ did not want to touch his hand. But she did, anyway.

As soon as they touched, she received an electrical charge and the buzzing intensified. She relaxed her shoulders and took a moment to rebuild her internal walls. She didn't want him creeping into her thoughts.

His speech slurred. Was he drunk on power? "I guess you are her-re to pay me the last payment?" He smiled showing a mouth full of silver teeth. He chuckled to himself and asked, "So wat's the password?"

XJ slunk back. The dizzying buzzing got stronger. Her mother didn't mention any password in her notes.

Is this dude trying to play me?

Al Bibliotecario kept smiling. "U seem sensitive. U block us out. Are u okay?"

XJ straightened her spine. It was as if every person in the motel was taking pot shots at her mind. Trying to rip her to shreds from the inside. But somewhere deep, she heard her mother's voice from her training— telling her about walking meditation, her mind cleared instantly.

"What password?" She said with attitude. "Stop screwing around." Would her mother have said that? She didn't know but her nerves were raw and she was sick.

Al Bibliotecario grinned again, and put a toothpick in his mouth. He cleared his throat, "Well, I check, u know. 'Ust in case u wer-re a spy or somethin'."

Whew! XJ relaxed even though her back was drenched in sweat.

She took the briefcase and threw the last of the cash on the living room coffee table. She wasn't getting close to him.

He sauntered over to the table and investigated the contents. "Why u want this infor-r-mation so bad?" His stuttering Spanglish was thick.

XJ felt the buzzing creeping back into her mind. She kept her cool. "None of your business." Her voice sounded hard even to her.

He took the money to his dining room table. The metallic stench floated up her nostrils. She gagged, but controlled it with a short cough.

"I hope my scent is getting to you, no?" he said. "It's been ve-r-ry strong since u've been help me keep my cell str-r-ong." He removed the toothpick and sucked his teeth. "Fear-r, it is motivator-r. I on't know how I will keep 'em under-r my control without you."

What is this freak talking about? She responded, "Not my problem."

"Oh, but it 'ill be." He took out this helmet and placed it on his head.

Was he threatening her? *Little prick.*

He gave her another creepy smile and offered his hand like he was a gentleman.

"U get close to me, hold my hand so I can put in your brain." He used his other hand to point to her. "No 'fraid. It's simp-ple."

XJ hesitated, narrowing her eyes. Her gut lurched as she walked over to him. He grabbed her hand and yanked her in like a queen bee. She wanted to run—hide—but she'd have to get this information. So she calmed down and focused on receiving.

"How does this work?" She stuttered, as she took a sudden intake of breath.

"Simple. Information bubble up into helmet." He tapped the helmet with his free hand. "I imprint to your brain then I give you disk to get code to unlock later-r. Now, come close."

XJ's eyes widened and her body jumped when she made contact. A surge of a million bees crawled up her arm. She shook.

Would he know that she wasn't her mom? She just wanted to get the information and go.

Al Bibliotecario kept rubbing her arm and pulling her closer. His face was close to hers while his arms touched her all over. Hive energy trapped her.

His eyes gazed deep into hers but he looked stupid with that helmet on his head. He moved to kiss her. She smashed her eyes shut. She wanted to push him off the step stool but she kept her mouth closed as his dried lips assaulted her. Between that metallic stench, and the powerful hive-like surge, XJ wanted to vomit.

Hazy images transferred into her mind with small, humming jolts. She couldn't figure out what they were but she opened her mind.

Numbers in a sequence ... and letters floated ... but she couldn't quite grasp them. Al Bibliotecario's hands moved to fondle her. Warning bells went off inside her head. His stench grew stronger and it felt like he was suffocating her with too much information too fast.

She tried to knock him down but she realized that she wouldn't be able to get all of the numbers and letters if she did that. Between the electrical charge and the images floating in her mind, she thought she would explode.

Her eyes popped open and Al Bibliotecario smiled, sinisterly. "U no get it all. Too good to lose." He said in his broken Spanglish. "U stay here, help me contr-rol my cell."

Is this guy joking? He must be nuts! Then XJ realized that he was trying to use subliminal mind control on her. It buzzed and burned inside her brain.

"Screw you!" XJ tried to break his grip. She still hadn't gotten all the information she needed. It seemed that he'd only passed her one full number—a number that she didn't understand.

She pushed back inside his mind. The experience was like pushing a sticky, telepathic liquid barrier. If he wouldn't give it to her, she would go inside and find it herself. She thought about her mother and the need to save her and threw her mind inside the hive mind.

She heard Al Bibliotecario gasp ... but she focused on finding out what she needed. She'd leapt into what looked like a surreal, virtual library with millions of books. She walked over to one and tried to take it but a jolt knocked her mentally and physically across the room.

She came to with him on top of her, with his fist closed to punch her in the face. The surreal moment sunk in as she saw his fist coming down. She rolled away from the path of the punch. She almost didn't make it because this body was too fat.

"U steal from me!" Al Bibliotecario looked wild-eyed.

The helmet crookedly sat on his head with wires dangling from the back. It looked like he'd ripped himself from his connection. He lifted his foot and tried to stomp her in the stomach. XJ rolled again and his foot crashed through the living room table.

"If you'd just given me the information that I paid for, and let me go we wouldn't have this problem!" XJ shouted as she tried to get out of his way.

"We could've be special but you steal from me!" Al Bibliotecario grabbed XJ by her braids and wrapped them around his fist, as he dragged her body over to the dining room table; and mashed her head down. It happened so fast, she didn't know what to do.

"I show u how, ke-ep beeches like u under control." He spat.

XJ squirmed but her head was on the table like it was being served. He was *strong*. He mashed her head on the table harder and it felt like her neck would snap. He was straddling her from behind. She had to get out of this vulnerable position. Was he going to rape her?

"Let's make a deal!" She screamed. "I keep helping you control your cell!"

XJ could see Al Bibliotecario's reflection in a nearby picture. He hesitated and then she realized that he meant to pound her head with his other fist.

His fist came down like a hammer on her temple and the pain raced through her body. She had to get away from him, but the weight of him holding her down, she couldn't get out.

"I no need you!" He said. "U took the babies so 'dey do 'wat I want."

XJ's stomached lurched. Did her mother actually do that? But she couldn't think of that. She took the moment to lift her high heel and donkey kick him as hard as she could. Al Bibliotecario stumbled back.

"Bruha!" He yelled and tried to leap on top of her again, but this time she was ready and moved out of his way.

XJ watched Al Bibliotecario crash. He caught his footing and reached for her. She tried to get away. He grabbed her. The skin to skin contact caused a surge. She tried to push him off. She was trapped.

His sinister eyes peered deep into hers as the sound of buzzing bees drowned her mind. Everything stopped. She couldn't tell if she were asleep or awake. All that remained was the static buzzing. Her vision looked like a kaleidoscope. Millions of bees buzzed within her mind, but she could see the faces of every soul connected to Al Bibliotecario.

"U die." XJ heard his voice. She couldn't move. A downpour of information assaulted her like a rolling avalanche. She silently screamed.

"Now u see the tr-rue power." Al Bibliotecario spit out. Her mind was like mush. Waves kept coming and coming and coming. Her mind gagged and choked.

Her mother's voice was a small whisper but XJ heard it. *Sweetheart let the information flow through you like a sieve.... Make your mind a sieve.*

"*Mom?*" But the voice was gone.

XJ let it flow. She became a conduit, then separated and became a watcher. Her mind's eye could see the situation, but her essence was protected.

The information flow stopped. Everything cleared and XJ settled back into her own mind. She could sense the cell members and Al Bibliotecario, but he'd exhausted himself. XJ began to erect her mental walls.

In a last effort, Al Bibliotecario stretched wide inside her mind and tried to drown her. XJ shielded her mind in a large bubble. His attacked bounced back.

XJ watched as he drowned inside his own information. Her eyes popped open and the buzzing had ceased. She looked up as Al Bibliotecario's whole body seized and collapsed on top of hers.

"Oh, my God!"

She pushed his limp body off and scooted back towards the wall. XJ shook uncontrollably. What should she do? She had to get out of here. Had she killed this man? She looked down at her hand and realized that her disguise was gone. She was back to herself.

She heard footsteps on the catwalk. She still didn't have the information that she needed but she had to get out of there. She grabbed Al Bibliotecario's helmet. Maybe there was still something left in there. She raced out of the room. When she got outside and on the steps she heard a shriek.

"No! She kill him! We never get our bebes!" She heard a female's voice in Spanglish. "*Find* her!" XJ was already down the three flights of steps and almost to her car.

She pulled out her car keys and jumped in.

When she looked back in her rear view mirror, she saw the residents all lined up on the catwalk, wailing and pointing to her car. She'd gotten away with one weird number but at least she was alive.

How was she going to extract anything from this helmet? She gunned the accelerator.

Chapter 39

"Sometimes, we all need a moment to take a breath."
—Xavier Patterson

Brandon sped down Rockbridge Road. He changed gears and mashed the accelerator. Everything pissed him off. Did XJ really slap him? He gripped the clutch tighter. It was easier for him to use his ability to drive but when he was mad, driving his Mustang calmed him.

He drove to Stone Mountain Park. His mother always took him to a special spot here. He needed to feel connected to her. He really missed her. He down-shifted and pulled off the road into a gravel lot.

It was after dark, but he didn't care if the park was officially closed. He pulled into a tree covered parking spot and turned off the engine. He cranked the car seat back and allowed his body to settle as he folded his arms tight. He wanted to scream, but he closed his eyes.

He dug XJ. Maybe she suspected that he was with Heather. *I should've been real with her and told the truth.*

But, until he figured what information Heather had, he didn't want to chance it. His soul cried out to find who ordered the murder of his mother. He wanted to take CAGE down. His stomach boiled, burned. What did his dad have to do with all of this?

He needed to rest then figure it out. He dropped into a deep, deep dream trance. Warmth filled his body. He was a younger version of himself and his mother was with him.

Her image was sunshine bright.... He could smell her perfume.... He was loved, safe, and secure....

"What's wrong?" He could hear the worry in her voice.

"Nothing, Mom. I just wanted to see you. I miss you." Brandon didn't want to alarm her.

"Silly. I'm always with you. She pulled him into her arms and rubbed his hair."

"How is your father?" she asked. "Is he well?" Brandon heard the hesitation in her voice.

"I guess he's fine." Brandon didn't know; didn't care.

"Well, how's my little race car driver?" she asked.

"Not so little anymore," he said. He wished he was still a baby, and that she was still alive.

He continued, "What if you loved someone, but you had to do something that you knew would hurt them, but it was for a good reason?"

"My son is in love." Her joy warmed him. "But, if you love then there should be no pain, no hesitation, no question."

His forehead scrunched up and he took a serious tone. "I think I found out why CAGE murdered you. But it will take me to do something that will hurt the girl I love."

His mother grew silent, continuing to stroke his hair. "My murder isn't something that you should worry about." His mother sat up and pulled his face so he could see her. He focused on her outline, blinded by her surreal image.

"CAGE is dangerous. Too much for you. I want you safe. Let your father handle it." He saw the worry in her eyes.

He turned away. "Dad's not interested. He could care less. He doesn't miss you like I do."

His mother pulled him into her arms. "My poor baby. You don't know how he hurts. I don't want you to do this. You are like your father, determined. It's hard for me to say anything that will stop you."

Brandon pulled back. "I am NOT like my father! He's the reason you're dead."

She soothed his back. "Yes, you are like him." His mother sounded resigned. "The two of you are made from the same cloth." She kissed his forehead. "But I will tell you. Your father loved me more than life itself. He would have done anything to keep me safe. He'll do anything to keep you safe."

Brandon wanted to argue but it was hard. She was always right. He kept listening to her. "I think what you seek, in searching for what happened to me, will end with you understanding your father better. But be careful. Don't lose the one you love in your quest for knowledge...."

His mother's image begin to fade as Brandon moved back into reality. Her words stung, but he had to find out what happened, why she was killed. It wouldn't let go of him. The coolness of the car made him shiver, as the memory of the k-bar dripping with her blood filled his mind. Whatever he had to do to figure this out, he would do it.

Brandon completely woke up and realized that he needed to see XJ. He pulled from underneath his covered spot, as daylight peered through his windows. He'd stayed at Stone Mountain Park all night, and now he felt calm as he drove.

He pulled up to XJ's house and put the car in park. He ran his fingers through his hair. He didn't want to lose her. He needed her. He felt connected to her, but he had to get information from Heather.

Should I just tell XJ the truth? Will she listen to me? Heather means nothing to me.

Something shattered his thoughts. *Is that XJ?* He squinted. *What the heck is she wearing? Looks like a suit, four sizes too big and a pair of high heels.* She was carrying a massive football helmet and she was crying.

He pushed out of his Mustang and bolted. By the time he'd reached her, she'd collapsed on the front porch in tears.

"What's wrong? Are you alright?" he asked, winded. He wanted to scoop her up in his arms, carry her in the house, and take care of her. But he stopped just short to give her space.

"No. I mean, yes. I'm fine. I just had a moment. I'll be okay." Brandon saw her wipe her tears on the back of her hand.

He moved closer cautiously. "Can I help you inside? I know you're mad at me, but you look like you need a friend."

He could see that she was shaken up. She answered weakly, "Don't you have a girlfriend to attend too? Don't worry about me."

Brandon wondered if she knew about Heather. "I don't have a girlfriend, yet. I was kinda hoping that you'd be my girlfriend." He moved closer to XJ and sat next to her on the porch. His arms desperately wanted to wrap around her and hold her, but he held back.

"Brandon, I know about you and Heather." Her nose sounded stuffy and she continued to shake. "Please, don't lie to me. I know you guys are together."

She did know about Heather! He was crushed. He hated Heather. He didn't want to be with her. He wanted XJ.

Brandon had to get this right. He slumped next to her. "Look ... Heather and I used to be together and it didn't work out. She's not the kinda girl that I like spending time with ... but for now I sorta have too."

XJ shivered. "Bull, Brandon! You promised that you'd help me and now you're off with the uppity white girl? What kinda crap is that?"

Brandon didn't want to hurt her, but he still had to see Heather. "Heather has information about my mother's murder. I have to play a game with her until she tells me." He could tell that that calmed her a little.

"Oh." Her voice sounded strange, awkward. "I understand. I didn't know."

They both sat in silence and Brandon scooted closer. He wanted to fold XJ into his body and take care of her. But he resisted. He wanted her to be his girlfriend, but with all this stuff going on with Heather, he didn't want to hurt her.

"I guess you can't help me then." She sounded wounded, lost. He hated that she sounded like that.

He turned to face her, touched her chin and looked deep into her eyes, "What do you need?"

He wanted to kiss her tears away. He wanted to protect her. He wanted to make her fears go away. He would do both. He had to find a way to help XJ and get the information from Heather.

XJ's eyes were beautiful and serious. "I have a number that I came across. I don't know what it means. Can you help me figure it out?" Her voice sounded weak.

He wanted to tell her how deeply he felt. Instead he said, "What's the number?"

Chapter 40

"Jealously in the GEP Revolution is dangerous."
—Dorothy Kates-Patterson

XJ wanted Brandon to hold her. Instead she pushed away, stood up and put some space between them. She trusted him ... a little. Her mom had such messed-up relationships with men, and she wanted to be free from male drama.

But her heart craved Brandon. She sensed his hand on her back and turned her body to resist his inviting arms. She opened the door.

His voice was a concerned whisper. "I want to help. Tell me the number. I promise to figure it out."

Her insides were jumbled. She wanted to hit him ... to tell him to get away from her ... and hold him. Instead she turned to face him.

"I shouldn't tell you this...."

His eyes stopped her. He was genuinely concerned. She wanted to pound his chest, to tell him how angry and jealous she felt. She didn't care if he was working his own story. When he was with Heather he looked like he was in, all the way. He looked like he enjoyed it. Her stomach twisted.

"How can I trust you? You have your own story. My mom's story is secondary," XJ said.

He took his hand and touched her face. Her insides twisted. *God, I want to kiss him so bad. I want him to hold me. I wanna feel safe in his arms.*

XJ watched his lips move closer. She froze. Her voice squeaked as she blurted. "200175312."

He stopped just short of kissing her. "What was that?"

"200175312. That's the number that I have. It keeps replaying over and over in my mind. I don't know what it could be, but it's very important to helping me with my mom."

XJ turned to open the front door of her house. Brandon moved close and hugged her from behind. Her stomach flip flopped.

His voice was close to her ear, "I'll help you XJ. Can you put it in my phone so I can access it anytime?"

She leaned into the front door, pushing it open, and entered the house. "Yeah, I can. Let me see it."

The moment their hands touched hot sparks flared. XJ couldn't control herself. He smelled wonderful and his beautiful eyes swallowed her whole. His arms opened and she fell into a hot kiss.

The kiss touched her deeply. Her body eased into it and then it became like breathing. It was intense, loving, and caring. She wanted to do more. She wanted to be more. She wanted more. She could feel Brandon's arms around her and she felt safe.

Then, XJ heard a buzzing noise.... Brandon kept kissing. She broke the kiss. "Brandon wait! What was that?"

He looked aggravated. "Nothing."

The jealousy crept back. "It's her isn't it?" She backed away folding her arms.

He didn't have to answer. She already knew it. She understood. If it were her mom she would do what was necessary. She hated Heather.

His voice stumbled, "Yeah. It's her. I better go. Type the number in here."

XJ snatched the phone from him and typed in the number that kept cycling through her mind. She didn't want him to go. She wanted him to stay. She wanted to tell him everything. More importantly, she wanted him to be her boyfriend.

Brandon scratched his head. "I promise I'll find this out for you." He kissed her forehead. She wanted to stop him—grab him, hold him back. But she let him go.

"I understand. Do what you gotta do. I'll work things on my end." She watched him walk away and closed the door. Her heart crushed.

Chapter 41

"Rich GEPs get away with anything!"
—Member, Humans United

Heather rolled across the desk some more.

"Idiots!" She yelled and threw the stapler at the door. "You can't keep me from Brandon! You can't keep me from the man I love!"

Heather screamed. It felt so good to scream! She felt empowered. The screaming released her anxiety. It was a therapeutic yell. Her hands shook some more. Someone had her purse and her pills. She needed a pill so *bad*.

Something inside her said that this was all bad—really bad for her, but she couldn't connect to that side. It felt like a hazy version of her mind. She could see herself inside her mind, like her true self. But then this was who she was ... wasn't it?

"Screw you people!" She yelled some more. "Screw all of you!" Screams felt so good! She wanted to scream again, but this time she leapt off the desk and used her strength to turn it over. She wanted to hurt someone for keeping her away from Brandon.

That's when she remembered. Brandon. He'd come for her. He'd save her. He'd love her. Something warmed inside and calmed her. She zeroed in on him and she realized that she still had her phone in her pocket. Her hands shook as she texted him.

I need you, now. Pick me up from school. He'd come for her now. He'd have to come. He'd have to love her.

She bashed herself in the head with the phone. "No! No! *No!* Stupid! He doesn't love you! Wake up!"

Who said that? Was that me?

Heather felt confused. She screamed more and more and more. She no longer had tears. All she could hear was the sound of her own screaming and it felt good. She could scream her confusion, horror, and frustration away.

Warm arms embraced her. The presence soothed her. The little voice inside her mind that was her true self, told her that the love of her life was there. Everything would be okay now. Her whole body relaxed. The screaming inside and outside stopped, with the warmth that smelled like home, comfort, and love all together....

Heather heard Saskia's calming voice, "It's okay Heather. I've got you. Calm down sweetie. I won't let them drive you insane."

Saskia? Heather wanted to bolt but the person deep inside told her to let Saskia love her. Soon the warmth of Saskia spread throughout her body and the calm overtook her. She felt Saskia's body cradling her ... her hands rubbed her hair ... her kisses touched her forehead, cheek, and face.

Heather released into her. It felt good. It felt right. It felt calm. The voice inside her told her that Saskia would help her survive this; and that those pills that Nadia had her taking were bad for her.

Heather scooted into Saskia more. Her body reacted. So many sensations at a time ... but with the confusion inside her, she knew that she wanted to love Saskia back ... she wanted to love her, hold her, kiss her and care for her back.

Heather felt like her true self was coming through. "Sas, I'm so sorry. I'm sorry."

"Shh ... it's alright." *Saskia soothed her and warmed her.* "We've got to get you out of here okay?"

"Okay." *Heather hesitated but she had to look Saskia in the eye.* "I love you, but I don't have control. It's the pills."

Saskia's eyes looked sad. "I know it's not you."

Saskia kissed her forehead and Heather couldn't control herself. She lifted her mouth, and kissed Saskia with her soul. Her mind and body felt electrified and connected. The kiss helped her connect to who she was for a split second. But it was gone again. She broke the kiss and moved back from Saskia. Calmer.

"Take me away from here, okay?" Heather pleaded with her. *"Take me away, so we can be together and alone."*

Tears rolled down Saskia's face. "I wish I could, sweetie. I wish I could."

Chapter 42

"Sometimes GEPs use their abilities to become their own enemies without knowing it."
—Saskia Milos

Brandon drove into the school's parking lot, parked in the back and got out—the place was crazy mad. CAGE vehicles, helicopters, and news crews made a circus at the front of the school. He wondered what the heck was going on. He put a hood over his head, and made his way into the eye of the frenzy, blending in with the crowd.

"Heather just went crazy and smashed Raven's face in." He heard a student say.

"Yeah ... they said Raven used her creepy powers on her." Another voice answered.

"Are you kidding? Heather is sprung on Brandon." Was it one he recognized?

"Brandon must be putting it on that girl. I wouldn't mind trying her out myself."

He scoffed at that comment. It came from a Hispanic classmate. *If he only knew, he wouldn't say that.*

"You NASTY!" a white girl with a ring in her mouth laughed.

The voices moved into the background. Brandon hid within the crowd. *Did Heather lose it like that?* He needed to find out more.

He was just opening the doors when a massive group of CAGE officers pushed him out of the way. He stumbled back.

His hood came off as he crashed into a group of students. The CAGE officers were bringing Heather out the door. She was hugging someone and her face was half-covered.

Her eyes met Brandon's. She looked empty.

Brandon's shoulders tightened. Her CAGE escorts stopped and all eyes focused on him. Before he could get out of the way, they grabbed him and dragged him into a separate vehicle. Brandon slumped in the back of the vehicle, his heart pounding. *It all happened so fast!*

He didn't know what to think or feel but he was curious. He'd never really seen the inside of a CAGE facility. Maybe this could work to his advantage.

He paced the floor. Seems like he'd been in the CAGE waiting room forever. Were they holding him? His pulse raced. The room was mind numbing with the pale green walls, stiff-backed, brown chairs with an institutionalized décor.

Brandon wanted to puke. He eyed the receptionist. He needed something to keep his mind busy. *If she would just leave!* He jumped in place and swung his arms around to loosen up.

Finally, the receptionist left her desk and took a break. He smiled and cracked his neck. Here was his chance to tap into CAGE's system.

He touched the cell phone in his pocket and accessed the numbers that XJ had given him. He had it in his mind's eye. Then he went over to the computer and touched it. This woman must have been a fool! She'd left the terminal open after she'd typed her password. It would be too easy for him to hack the system.

Brandon closed his eyes, tapped into his technopathic ability and began to tunnel through the system. It felt odd, being able to freely manipulate the system. He was used to hacking in. He found the receptionist's access codes and stored them in his phone. These might come in handy again.

Now he made the keyboard type XJ's number. *It has to mean something.... I found it!*

It was a case number for a girl named Amber being held in Zone 6. Brandon quickly used his ability to download all the information to his phone, and forwarded it to XJ.

Something good had to come from playing this game with Heather. Now I'll see what I can find out about my mom.

Brandon used his mind's eye to make the keyboard type his mother's name. He followed the trail of information, but hit a firewall inside his head.

His stomach lurched. Suddenly, his mind went cloudy as a virus tried to rewrite his brain. He pulled out but the bio-virus kept following him. Fear crept along his spine. He'd thought he was safe and didn't take his usual precautions.

He had to outrun the thing before it caught up with him! With lightening speed, Brandon exited from the connection and fell back from the computer. His heart was racing and he was mentally exhausted. He passed out.

Brandon opened his eyes. He was surrounded by CAGE officers.

"Did you have a good trip?" the receptionist asked.

He had trouble focusing. "Excuse me?"

She put her face close to his. "Did you have a good trip when you were hacking into my workspace?"

Brandon bit his lower lip. *How am I going to get out of this? Will my dad help me this time?*

"I—I don't know what you mean!" He tried to sound sincere.

"Cut the bull! You know, we totally set you up and you bit. The only thing we have to do now, is figure out what you touched. It's so hard to track you people." The receptionist walked over and began to click the keys on her keyboard.

Brandon worried that he'd left a trail. And then it dawned on him. The virus was a tracker! He rubbed his hands through his hair.

Was I really that dumb? Why didn't I see it?

The receptionist popped in a flash drive and copied something. "Got it!" She smiled at him. "Take him away!"

Brandon threw a punch at the oncoming CAGE officers, but missed. He couldn't go out like this. He jumped up and tried to fight them. But they pushed him down and a big knee pierced his back. He tried to buck up, but there were too many of them.

"Do you know who my father is?!" he screamed. "He won't let you take me like this!" His heart pounded in his ears, as they put plastic cuffs on his hands and forced him up.

The receptionist smiled. "That certainly didn't stop us from neutralizing your mother, now did it?" Her words punched him in the gut. He couldn't breathe.

The CAGE officers dragged Brandon out of the room. He sunk his head low. As they reached the door, he saw pink high heels.

Heather said, "Let him go!"

The CAGE officers stopped and looked at the receptionist. She began to explain, "Miss Stillwell, we caught this young man hacking into our system and you know the rules about...."

"*Shut* up!" Heather looked cleaned up, like she was back to her old self. "You know you set him up." The receptionist slung her brown hair back like she was in control, but her face looked pale.

Heather's freshly manicured, perfect pink finger pointed at the CAGE officers, with a sense of confidence and power. "Brandon is the love of my life, and none of you will stop us from being together! Let him go!"

The CAGE officers cut Brandon loose, and shoved him out of the way. He straightened out his outfit.

"Come here Brandon." Heather held out her hand. "I need you on my arm to escort me out of this place."

He attached himself to Heather's arm, relaxed his shoulders and took a deep breath. They walked away together with their heads held high.

When they rounded a quiet corner, she turned to him and said, "Brandon Miller, you now owe me. I just saved your butt. You have a little news conference to attend. And you'd better act like you love me or I'll turn you back over to them."

Brandon stared at her. *What have I gotten myself into this time?*

Chapter 43

"Betrayal scorches the heart and soul of Revolution."
—John Brockman

XJ twirled around on the lab chair. She thought about Brandon. *Can I trust him?*

That had been her mother's problem, but she decided that it wouldn't be hers. *I refuse to be the revolutionary with a ka-zillion boyfriends. I don't want to get information that way. Did mom really love all those men?*

XJ felt confused. She knew she had deep feelings for Brandon. Did she love him? What kind of relationship could they have together?

Her phone beeped. It was a text from him. He'd come through with the number! *How did he get this intel?*

XJ hopped off the chair and walked over to Dr. Kates, who was using mechanical arms to retrieve the information from the helmet. "Granddad, I think I've got some information." She was happy to finally have *something*.

"OK, doll, connect it up over there ... and let's see what you've got."

XJ walked over and hooked it up to the super-computer. She caught a glimpse of her high school on the TV news.

"Granddad, how do I turn this up?" She pointed to one of the TVs on a bank of newscasts around the world.

The sound increased. "How's that?" Dr. Kates asked. XJ gave an affirmative nod and focused on the newscast.

"The follow-up on the story at Stone Mountain GEP High, Heather Stillwell, daughter to Nadia Stillwell, the Director of the Region V CAGE facility. Heather has had some sort of nervous breakdown at the school which involved another student."

"What has that uppity, white girl done now?" XJ mumbled.

The newscast continued. *"We're here in front of the Region V CAGE facility, waiting to hear the official word from the Director. Oh wait, here she comes."*

She watched the TV reporters swarm Nadia, and allowed the anger to fill her belly. Nadia looked dressed to kill in her red suit. She had that stuck-up, but dignified look, with her red lips, supermodel build, red pumps, perfect blond hair and blue eyes.

XJ hated her for stealing away her father, and even more for detaining her mother. Nadia always seemed to be at the center of her problems.

She listened and watched. Heather looked identical to her mother, except she was in hot pink. *How creepy is this? They really are the perfect Stepford family. How did he marry that woman? Me and dad don't fit with them at all. What's up with that?*

XJ laughed, *maybe I'd fit if I dyed my hair blond and only wore magenta.* Maybe then, she could get this kind of attention from news crews about what was going on with her mom. She turned to see her grandfather watching the newscast. They both looked on in silence.

Nadia spoke, *"I don't know why you are all here. My daughter had a little tiff at school. Hardly anything for the national news."*

The reporters yelled, *"Nadia, they said that your daughter severely disfigured another student, because she was jealous over a boy. Is this true?"*

Nadia fielded the question like an old pro. *"Of course not— that young woman is fine. And my daughter is just a teenager in love. Ah, here she comes now."*

Cameras snapped as Heather strutted and clicked in her hot pink heels. Confident, beautiful, and attractive. XJ let out a disgusted huff.

Nadia's red gloved hand point as she continued, *"As you can see, my daughter is fine. She's normal, happy, and stable. Aren't you dear?"*

Heather widened her phony smile for the cameras and waved. Then she spoke sincerely, as if she really meant it. *"I'm sorry for the confusion and I sincerely apologize for my part at school. I never imagined that my teen problems would make it on national news."*

XJ's stomach flip-flopped in disgust. She despised Heather too. *That trick is lying!* She watched Heather try to play it off.

But the reporters were relentless. *"What about the boy that you broke up with? Are you back together now?"*

Heather held her head back, while her blond curls bounced. She gave an entitled, rich laugh. *"You guys are so silly! Brandon is here and I can assure you that we're together."*

XJ's heart dropped as Brandon walked out proudly and stood next to Heather.

Her mouth fell open, as she watched Heather gaze lovingly into Brandon's eyes and they kissed on National TV for everyone to see. XJ's body recoiled and her shoulders slumped. She felt stupid, cheated, defrauded.

How could Brandon do this? Was this a part of the act?

She knew now, that she couldn't be in a real relationship with Brandon. They couldn't be together. Not only was it illegal but it was impractical. He stood up there on TV with his pink, perfect Blondie. They looked like they belonged together. They looked like they fit. Same mate-designation type. Same class. Same race.

XJ had hoped it wasn't true, but reality had set in. She refused to cry or stand there feeling foolish.

To make matters worse, Brandon spoke, *"Heather and I are a couple. We had a little disagreement but everything is okay. It's a little weird for all of America to be in the middle of our teenage spat, but we are together."*

XJ folded her arms. She wanted to scream. But instead, she turned away from the screen.

I will not cry!

Dr. Kates looked sympathetic. "I'm sorry, doll. I know you really liked that young man."

She could hardly breathe as she balled up her fists and released them. Feelings of betrayal overwhelmed her. She didn't think she'd ever trust Brandon again.

Heather's voice droned on in the background. *"I hope everyone will come see me and Brandon at the Miss GEP High School Pageant. We'll be a lovely couple."*

XJ wanted to wipe the smug expression off her step sister's face. She barely heard her grandfather when he told her that the file contained a photo of her first cousin. XJ straightened up and focused. She marched over to the terminal and looked into the face of the girl that she'd seen at the CAGE facility.

It's Amber!

XJ bit her lip as she realized that she wouldn't be like her mom and depend on a man. She wouldn't wait for Brandon the betrayer. Let him stay with his pink, blondie surprise. She would break into the CAGE facility and free her cousin all by herself.

She needed a plan.

Chapter 44

"The GEP Revolution is filled with lies and strange alliances. Nothing is as it seems."
—Xavier Patterson

Heather felt confident. She had her stride back. The right personality was in control. A wide grin spread across her face. Brandon had done wonderfully at the news conference. Now no one would question the love that they held in their hearts.

Fraud! her other voice clamored.

She stumbled. She wouldn't allow the *other* Heather to take away her victory. Her hands shook as she looped her arm in Brandon's. It felt natural to walk like lovers. They were perfect together.

"I'm so glad you're here with me. Everything will work out fine now." Heather gushed and puckered her lips in a playful kiss.

She gazed up at Brandon. His face was unreadable. It looked flat, expressionless. "Did you hear me? I love you, Brandon!" She stopped to make him look at her ... studying his perfect eyes, face, mouth. Her heart swooned.

Liar! the *other* Heather railed. *You don't love him!* She felt perspiration roll down her back. Her hands trembled. "Shut-up!" she whispered.

Heather moved closer to Brandon and stood up on her toes to kiss him. He shrank away, making her miss her mark.

"You won't get away!" She forced him down to her size and planted an awkward kiss. The magic didn't materialize.

The *other* Heather said, "You're an idiot!"

Brandon abruptly broke the kiss. "Really? Did you forget that I owe you?"

Her heart jumped. The voice inside her laughed crazily. Heather couldn't stand it—her body shivered.

"Shut up! Shut up!" She pounded her head and bent over. Then, she forced herself to stand straight up. A part of her wanted to believe that deep down inside he really did love her—and want her, but it was a lie.

Why doesn't he love me? Rage formed in the pit of her stomach. "After all I've done for you—you better act like you love me! Kiss me again, like you mean it!"

Heather saw Brandon's movements in slow motion. He pushed her back, put his face down close to hers and lowered his voice. "I don't love you!" he hissed poisonously. "Get a clue!"

Heather screamed and reached up to claw his beautiful face. Her hunter abilities turned on and her vision went red. He grabbed her hands. *The tears would not stop!* The mocking laughter inside her head would not stop! *The tremors would not stop!*

She had to leave, so she yanked away, whirled around and marched into the nearest restroom. *How dare he not want me? Doesn't he know who I am?*

Anyone would be glad to have her as a girlfriend, lover or mate. Heather went into the stall, slammed the toilet seat down and plopped down on the toilet. She ripped toilet paper from the spool and let the tears flow.

The *other* voice inside told Heather that Brandon was right. And she didn't love him either. She loved someone else, but the real her was being suppressed. She wiped her eyes.

This bathroom smells awful! She would tell the custodians to do a thorough cleaning job.

She bent over and put her elbows on her thighs. This was all such a mess! At least she felt calm now. Heather heard the door creak open as someone entered the restroom. She stood up to crack the stall door.

OMG! She looked at urinals and realized that she was in the men's bathroom.

The people walking in were her doctors. Heather clicked the door shut and pulled her legs up so they wouldn't know she was there listening.

"That went well." A voice she didn't recognize said. She heard pants unzipping and urine hit the back of the urinal.

"Yes, it did." That sounded like Dr. Robinson.

"I feel sorry for that little girl," the first voice said.

Who are they talking about?

She heard the water running, then Dr. Robinson asked, "Is there anyone here?"

Both men looked underneath the stalls and then they locked the door. The first voice said, "What Nadia is doing to her daughter is unforgivable—drugging her like that! Are you sure she'll be alright?"

Dr. Robinson sounded thoughtful, "The intermixing of the drugs, with the girl's unique abilities has made her the perfect tracker."

"Will that microscopic chip you inserted in her shoulder work?"

Dr. Robinson hesitated. "I don't know.... It's set to release medicine whenever the wrong personality takes control of her thoughts. It treats the real personality like a virus."

"It's a good solution." The other voice said proudly.

"It releases in the dosage that correlates to the strength of the primary personality. I don't know what will happen if the primary tries to come back strong." Now Dr. Robinson sounded worried.

Heather scrunched down and peered under the stall, watching Dr. Robinson as he scratched his head and adjusted his glasses. "To be able to program her to focus on the one target is a breakthrough.

But the real girl is lost. I don't know what the long term affects will be. It may lead to permanent, multiple personalities or schizophrenia."

Heather slumped back on the toilet, stunned. She shook her head. *This can't be true! Would my mother really do that to me?* Was it because she was adopted? *Dr. Robinson must be lying!*

"Nadia must want that TV producer under her control very badly—to make him her daughter's target. It's just wrong. We could've used a number of other operatives." The other man sounded as if he knew something. But could his words be trusted?

Heather felt confusion, anger, and frustration take over.

She was lost.

Dr. Robinson said, "Well, we know Nadia is willing to do whatever it takes to get what she wants, even drugging and prostituting her own daughter."

Heather felt the meltdown start. This time that voice inside helped her. She held it together as one person. She heard them exit, then she came out.

The voice inside her mind said, *We can never trust mother again.* Heather put her hands on her hips, as she peered at her image in the mirror. "I agree."

But what would she do now?

Chapter 45

"When you stand up on your own two feet, it feels like you're breaking free from everything."
—XJ Patterson

XJ stepped out of the government vehicle as Joanne Chesimard. She'd decided to take matters into her own hands. Since all of the news crews were hanging around like propaganda vultures, she figured she could slip in and save her cousin without notice.

CAGE would not be on alert. She had between two to three hours before her disguise wore off. Just in case, she brought a purse she'd found with Joanne Chesimard's belongings.

It had a CAGE security key card, a small mini tablet PC, a make-up case, and a change of clothes that XJ added. She figured that would be enough.

XJ's heart pounded like crazy. She was scared—really scared. She thought about the last time she'd left CAGE, unconscious, and the torture that they'd put her through. But she pushed it out of her head. As her mother would say, there was no sense in dwelling on defeat.

She concentrated on her main goal: rescuing her cousins, and then saving her mother. Her sensible pumps clicked as she walked.

I can do this! She could play the social worker. She took out Chesimard's card and placed it on her jacket; walked up to the employee entrance and went inside.

One of the CAGE guards said, "Ms. Chesimard, please step this way. It's been a while since you've been here—you must debrief."

XJ's heart pounded. Sweat poured down her back. What was this debriefing thing? She'd have to improvise.

She stammered in the unfamiliar voice. "Sure—Sure, I'm ready to debrief."

The guard escorted her into a small room off to the side. The room looked like a psychiatrist's office with gray walls, book shelves, and a security camera that was almost hidden, but obvious to XJ. She sat down in the only chair in front of the camera.

A mechanical voice sounded, *"Welcome, Joanne Chesimard. It's been eight days since your last check-in. You were working on Case Number 2015-7819, What has been your progress?"*

XJ's squeezed her fingernails into her palms, her nerves rattled. *I got to keep cool. But what can I do? What is case number 2015-7819?*

She thought for a moment and then said, "No progress or updates to report."

The mechanical voice said, *"Noted. Please exit to the rear of the room and to your assigned area."*

The door swooshed and popped open. XJ's shoulders released. She smiled inwardly. *That was easy.*

XJ walked to the door and into an office area. She had no idea where her desk was located. She kept going, trying not to look nervous until she found her name plate and sat down.

She almost burst into tears. There, on the desk, was her mom's stuff or at least stuff that looked like her mom would have. It looked like her mother had worked as Joanne Chesimard for years! There were certificates of excellence, and other office paraphernalia.

XJ saw her mother's computer and began to type. What would her log-on be? She typed her own name and it worked. She began to search through the system. She had to find her cousin.

Occasionally, she looked behind her to see if anyone noticed her. But so far the place was relatively empty. It looked like everyone was busy elsewhere.

Here it is! She'd found Amber's file, but XJ realized that she'd have to retrieve her from Zone 6. She put in a requisition to have the girl brought down. *Ziggy's here, too....*

She put in another requisition to have him brought down. XJ bit her bottom lip again, and glared at the clock. She should be able to rescue them in an hour from the pick-up area, if she knew where it was. Her nerves rattled again. She was really scared but this *had* to be done.

XJ looked around, trying to figure out which one of the rooms was the pick-up area. Then she saw the sign. *OMG, what will I do for an hour? I need to look like I'm working!*

She started to look at her mother's case files, and found Ector's file. *What did Mom do with those children? Did she really take them to Zone 6?*

XJ was so engrossed in the research, that she didn't hear someone come up behind her.

The voice made her stomach wrench.

"Joanne, so good of you to join us for our meeting." It was Ms. Hughes, the social worker who tortured her.

XJ's jaw and heart dropped.

"I saw your update about the Information GEPs which wasn't much. You'll need to do some more explaining." The social worker looked really serious. XJ glanced at the clock behind her, and knew that she didn't have time for an interrogation from this woman.

She heard Joanne's voice come out of her mouth. "I'm busy. Can this wait?"

Ms. Hughes showed her a gold tooth grin. "Gurl, you know I love you." XJ watched the chubby brown hand move to pat her on the back, and tried not to flinch. "But, I've got to do my job just like you do."

XJ studied Hughes's face. In the office light, the woman looked like an old, worn-out purse. Her deep-set, brown eyes had dark marks under them. And her short bob looked overly processed on the sides. The woman was balding.

Hughes pushed her face closer to XJ's. "We've been friends for years. You know I like your work. You get results. I just wanna know how you did it. How did you break those information GEPs? Tell me about case 2015-7819. I wanna know your secret."

XJ wanted to jump back from the woman like she'd seen a rattlesnake. She wanted to vomit. She glanced up at the clock again, and gave Hughes a big, fake smile. "Really ... can it wait say, 25 minutes?"

The social worker laughed. "Get your butt in interview room two."

What can I tell this woman? This isn't good.

XJ sat in the interview room. At least she could see the reflection of the clock in the two-way mirror. She only needed to play along for 20 minutes, and when she saw them bring down her cousin and Ziggy, she would jet. Maybe she could make up some sort of lie or just say she had to go to the bathroom.

The social worker sickened her. She couldn't believe that her mother was friends with this lady. *Definitely creepy!*

Her nerves were raw. She rang her hands underneath the table. If she could hold on for a few minutes, she would have a part of what she needed to save her mom and her family. XJ brought up her purse and put it in her lap.

You can do this. You can do this.

Ms. Hughes came in with her creepy, gold-tooth smile. Was this woman for real? She got her kicks from hurting people. XJ peered at the two way mirror again. She could also see the holding room. Maybe they would bring them early.

"Joanne," the social worker began. "This has been so unlike you. I had to cover for you with the Patterson girl, and I've been trying to reach you for several days. Is there something I should know about?"

XJ closed her eyes and took a deep breath. *Stay calm.* She opened her mouth, and heard Joanne's voice say dryly. "I've had a few family problems that I didn't want to bother you with." She gave the woman a half smile.

"Oh, well you do know the policy. CAGE social work must come first." The woman sounded genuinely concerned. Was this the same witch who tortured her?

"You've been my top social worker for years," Hughes continued. "Your record is exemplary. I can't believe that I'm having to counsel you. I—I just thought something happened to you."

The social worker reached over and rubbed her hand.

XJ jumped back like she was getting too close to a pit bull. She shrank in her seat; then glanced passed the social worker into the two-way mirror to see if CAGE had brought down Amber and Ziggy.

Not yet! She wet her lips.

"Are you sure you're okay?" Ms. Hughes droned on about how social workers could get in trouble, and what kinds of CAGE services were available. Her hands thumped against the table and XJ jumped. She wanted to scream. All she could remember was this woman inside her mind torturing her.

XJ cleared her throat. "Y—yes I'm fine. I just needed a little time to get some things together."

"Well, not to be cruel, but I need your report about the Information GEPs. What happened over there? Did that man attack you? We had to send in a clean-up crew." The social worker paused awkwardly, and waited for a response.

XJ's pulse thumped in her ears, as sweat rolled down her back. She glimpsed something in the two way mirror, and turned her whole body around to check it for sure.

It's them! Both Amber and Ziggy were being escorted into the holding room.

She breathed deeply, calming herself. "I promise to give you a full report. It was an awful, um … situation. I just need time to get my thoughts together." XJ stood up and smiled down at the woman.

"Joanne are you sure you're okay? You're looking a little flushed. Do you need some water?" Ms. Hughes showed more fake concern and reached out to touch XJ.

That's when she realized her disguise was wearing off.

She had to go *now.*

"N—no thank you. I just need to go to the restroom." XJ jumped up and the chair crashed.

She felt it. The social worker was snaking into her mind. She had to get out of here! She began to erect mental barriers. She could feel Hughes' compulsion, but this time she knew what to look for and blocked it. XJ had learned that she could push back telepathically and that's what she did.

Ms. Hughes collapsed back into the chair with wide eyes, and head rolling back. Her big jewelry, black pants suit pulled tight around her slumped form. She'd be passed out for at least a minute.

XJ scrambled out of the room, and raced towards the holding cell. She reached Amber and Ziggy and began to talk loudly, but professionally. "Alright, it's time to go! Get your stuff and let's move *quickly!*"

Amber and Ziggy cringed back when they saw her. "Wh— Where are you taking us?" Ziggy asked. "Are you going to kill us?" Her cousin had the same look of terror.

She had to calm them both down and her sweating was getting to be too much. She wiped her brow. *I've got to get them out of here!*

"Don't worry. Everything will be fine." Smiling, she pushed them out the door. "XJ will be waiting for you guys." They didn't look pleased or happy, but at least they got moving.

Someone behind her screamed.

XJ looked back and saw Hughes stumble out of the interview room, wheezing heavily. "I—I know that mind! It's not Joanne's at all! It's the Patterson *girl.*"

Oh no! Her pulse hammered as XJ ushered the two out into the hallway. Her disguise was bubbling, oozing off. She felt light-headed. *I can't pass out here!*

Her whole body rattled and shook. "Not now!" She yelled outloud and keeled over.

"Oh *God!* What's going on? Are you alright?" Amber's voice was in her ear.

But she couldn't talk. The transformation was taking her down. Hopefully, they could get somewhere safe.

"Let's go in here...." Amber said and XJ felt herself being shoved into a restroom. She screamed again, as her body bowed to the transformation. This was the worse change of all! Her body ached and her head felt like it had caved-in. She could feel the convulsions taking over. Her grandfather had never warned her about the effects of changing frequently.

The convulsing finally stopped, and her vision cleared. She looked up into Ziggy's face.

"*XJ!*" Ziggy yelled. He pulled her into a crushing hug.

"Ziggy let me *go!* The room is still spinning!"

"I *knew* this was weird!" Amber said. "Aren't you the girl from the hallway?"

Ziggy kept hugging her. "I'm so glad it's you! I missed you!" he said over and over in his rapid pace. "I missed you! I'm so glad it's you!"

She rubbed his hair, but her attention was on Amber. Her cousin had a butter-cream skin color, long black hair; and a tall, thin frame like hers. She was plainly dressed, but beautiful. Something about the girl's eyes looked familiar too. She'd found her first cousin.

"Yes, I'm that girl," XJ said smiling, "and more important you're my cousin."

Amber looked shocked. "My—my family? They left me! Are you *sure?*"

They heard screams and yells outside. XJ pushed Ziggy back, leapt up, and peered out the restroom door.

She started to talk fast. "We have got to get out of here before they catch us! I don't have a plan 'b' so we have to make another way."

Amber stood up and her finger transformed into a funny key, while her body went silently mechanical. XJ watched her stick her finger in the computerized bathroom door lock and the door clicked. The door and wall changed red and a series of letter and number codes steamed across the wall.

Somehow, her cousin had created a force field with her finger.

"That ought to hold them for a minute!" Amber pulled her finger out and stood back. "My cousin...," she said in a matter of fact voice. "Well, let's figure out a way to get out of here."

Chapter 46

"I—I'm not a part of no GEP Revolution. I—I'm just XJ's friend. Plu—ease don't hur—rt me. OU—UCH!"
—Ziggy in Zone 6

As Brandon rounded the corner, he heard screams. He rushed to find out what was happening. From what he could tell, the entire social work office was standing around one woman. He inched closer to hear.

The woman screamed. "She's *killed* her! She's killed Joanne! Get away from me! Let me call the CAGE officers!"

He heard shocked, muffled voices. Someone must have asked the woman what she was talking about and he heard, "XJ Patterson has killed Joanne Chesimard and—and has taken on Joanne's form! I don't know how she did it! She must be some form of chameleon! But she's obviously killed Joanne!"

Shocked gasps went through the crowd. Then he heard a male voice say, "Where are they?"

The woman answered, "The stupid revolutionaries ran into the bathroom. How could a child so young commit murder? Her mother probably put her up to it! We have to do *something.*" Screaming, the woman leapt up and started to pound the door.

Brandon let the shock fill him ... then he realized that he had to take action. He ducked into an office and attached his mind to the first workstation. He used the pass code from the receptionist. He knew it was booby trapped but he could anticipate it now. He quickly expanded his mind and dropped into CAGE's system. He had to slow down the CAGE officers to give XJ a chance to escape.

Suddenly he stopped, pulse pounding. With a jolt he realized that it had been *XJ* at the mall and not Joanne Chesimard.

She saw me with Heather! No wonder she smacked me! His heart hurt, but he had to focus and save her now.... *Found it!*

He completely re-routed the directions to mobilize. His senses told him that the virus was closing in. He backtracked out and went into another network to throw the tracking virus off.

Brandon began to try to search for information on his mom again, to allow the virus to catch-up with him. He realized, as dangerous as this was, that he was actually having fun. He played around inside CAGE's firewall, until he felt someone's hands grab his body physically—automatically disconnecting him.

Pain seared through his mind at the abrupt break in the connection. He doubled over.

He tried to see, but it took a minute for his vision to clear. Finally, he glimpsed a pair of pink shoes. It was Heather.

Brandon glared at her. "Wh—What are you doing? Are you some sort of idiot? What part of tracking virus don't you understand?" Heather looked around like she was a little nervous, but she talked low. She was acting weird.

Brandon raked his hands through his hair, and tried to reattach his mind to the terminal. "Heather, this is what I do. I'm a revolutionary. This is the man that you claim to love. Accept it."

Heather blew her breath out, and sat down next to Brandon. "I ... I don't know if I love you Brandon ... I don't know what to think."

He glanced over, as the commotion with the social work department became more heated. The workers were trying to get into the bathroom. It looked like XJ had the door barricaded.

I so don't have time to be listening to Heather's crap. He had to help the woman he loved. "What are you talking about?" Brandon tried to reconnect again.

Heather stopped him. "No, Brandon. I know you want to save your girlfriend. You need to use this code." She logged the other profile off and logged back in with a special code. "This one will give you lot's more access. Don't worry it's not connected to either one of us."

Now, he didn't know what to think. Who was this girl? It was like she was *different*. It freaked him out. He looked into Heather's eyes, but it was as if someone else peered out at him. Freaky, absolutely, freaky.

He dropped in quickly. This time he shut down the entire security system grid so XJ could find another way out. At least he *hoped* that's what she'd do.

As soon as he'd dismantled the system, a mechanical voice announced, *"Security grid offline. Will be activated in seven minutes."*

Well he'd done all he could do. XJ was smart, sexy and savvy. She'd figure out a way to escape. He slowly backed out of the system and re-entered his physical body.

Heather slapped his face. "How *dare* you use me like this?"

Brandon stared at her. *Didn't she just give me the code? The girl looks like she's coming apart.* Her eyes were wide and dilated.

"I can't believe you saved her! After everything I've done for you!" Heather leaped on top of Brandon and tried to scratch his eyeballs out.

She is definitely insane. "Heather get *off* me!" he yelled. "What the hell is wrong with you?"

"You can't have us both Brandon! You just *can't!*" Heather sounded out of breath. He grabbed her hands and held her there. He wouldn't let her hurt him, but he knew something wasn't quite right.

This was the Heather he remembered.

Chapter 47

"My three granddaughters are special. Each one has abilities that no one has seen. Together they are a force to fear."

—Dr. Gary Leonard Kates

"What *are* you?" XJ breathed. She'd seen lots of GEP abilities but nothing like this.

Amber smiled and she saw a family resemblance. Although she and her cousin had completely different skin tones, they had the same nose, chin, and eyes. Genetics didn't play.

"The official term is a technopathic changeling. I can interface with any electronic entity, by using a part of my body as a mechanical connector." She sounded like a geek.

"Deep...." XJ looked down at her outfit. "I look like a clown. I need to change."

Amber picked up her purse, rummaged through it and retrieved the small computer. "A-ha! This is what I need!"

Meanwhile, XJ went into a stall to change her clothes. When she came out she gasped. Amber was sitting on the floor with her head mechanically melded with the wall. She had the minicomputer attached to her hand like she was a cog in a big machine!

Ziggy grinned. "Isn't she beautiful?"

XJ caught her breath. "Is this *normal?* I mean it's freaky to say the least!"

"Don't worry. I'm still all here." Amber replied. "It was just easier for me to connect with everything this way ... I'm sort of a mix between human and robot."

She shook off her fear. After all, she had some weird abilities, too. "Can you find a way for us to get out of here?"

Suddenly, the lights went out.

"Did you do that?" XJ asked looking worried.

"No, it looks like someone has dropped a virus in the system." Amber sounded mechanical.

"OMG! Amber disconnect before the virus catches you!"

"It's okay." Amber said in her mechanical voice. "This is just what we need to get out. I've found an exit. Downloading now."

XJ relaxed a bit. Then, they heard a CAGE mechanized voice. *"System will be back online in five minutes."*

Someone started banging on the door again. "You little murderer!" It was Hughes. "You won't get away with this!"

XJ's heart pounded. *That social worker is really mad. It's funny, she thinks I murdered Joanne Chesimard. But Joanne is really my mother being held prisoner in Zone 6.*

As she watched Amber disconnect from the wall and the minicomputer, her entire movement seamless and liquid, XJ thought about how weird her family really was.

Ziggy started to hop around. "Ziggy, calm down." He was making her more nervous.

"I—I'm so sorry sorry XJ. I'm ... I'm just all wound up," Ziggy said at his lightening speed pace.

Amber walked over to the vent on the wall. "We can use the shaft to get out. It'll lead us to the front doors and a little room. We'll just have to walk out the front door though."

XJ sensed Amber's uncertainty, and she was feeling a little uneasy herself.

All at once, she heard her mother's voice in her head. *Take the chance child. Sometimes revolutionaries go with the hand they've been dealt.*

She called out inside her mind. *Mom, is that you?* But nothing came back.

A mechanical CAGE voice intoned. *"System will be online in four minutes."*

They had to get out of there.

XJ jumped up on the ledge and pried the metal plate off the wall. She threw it on the floor. That's when she felt the social worker trying to snake inside of their minds, but it was faint.

Amber said, "My firewall is keeping her out, too. Just ignore it."

XJ pulled herself into the shaft and slid inside and Ziggy lost it. I—I'm not going in there! I—I could die or something! *N—No way!* I can't get in there!"

"Ziggy take my hand," XJ urged. "I'll help you. This is our only way." She could see his mind churning and she pushed him with her abilities.

He reached for her hand and she pulled him up and into the shaft. Amber followed. The shaft was dark and they heard a muffled version of the mechanical voice. *"The system will be back online in three minutes."*

Amber's voice shattered her impending fear. "Crawl to the right and then to the left!"

XJ crawled quickly, but she heard Ziggy behind her. He was breathing hard and hyperventilating. Something inside her mind jumped. She realized that she could communicate with Ziggy mind to mind!

She called to him. *Ziggy we're almost out.*

He'd heard her. *X-XJ is that you?*

She sent him warm thoughts. *We'll be out soon, just keep crawling.*

O—OK. I love you XJ. Ziggy really was her best friend. XJ didn't know what she'd do without him.

Amber's voice was a whisper. "Turn left, but be quiet, we're right by the CAGE guard station."

XJ turned left and the CAGE mechanical voice announced, *"The system will be back online in two minutes."*

The voice spooked Ziggy and he lost it. He started shaking and sweating. XJ tried to calm him down, but she couldn't.

"I-I can't do it X—XJ! I-I'm not G-Gonna make it!" Ziggy started to crawl to the nearest exit.

"Ziggy, *no!*" XJ hissed. "You'll get yourself killed! We're almost out!"

Before she could grab him, Ziggy kicked open the vent and fell out.

XJ froze in shock. What should they do?

She saw the words in Amber's mind. *We've got to keep moving!*

She wanted to go after him. But there was no way to help Ziggy if they all got caught. The CAGE mechanical voice said, *"The system will be online in 58 seconds."*

Amber pointed towards the next right. They crawled like crazy—kicked the vent open and jumped out into a storage area.

"It's okay," Amber comforted her, "maybe we can find a way to help him later."

Fighting back the tears, XJ struggled to pull herself together.

At that moment, the system came on. *"System back online Alert! Alert!"*

The lasers inside the shaft went red and wild. But at least they were out of the shaft.

Now, they had to get out of the room.

Chapter 48

"I don't care what I have to do. Once I have the code, I will be queen of the GEPs. Humans United won't figure it out until it's too late. They won't stand a chance."
—Red Death

Heather couldn't believe how ungrateful Brandon was! She'd cared for him; looked out for him; loved him; and he repaid her by saving that jungle bunny, step sister of hers! The anger swirled inside. She tried to move her hands so that she could scratch his beautiful eyes out but Brandon held her tight.

She laughed from deep in her belly. This situation was hilarious. She just kept laughing and laughing and laughing. She heard the other voice inside her mind, but it was fuzzy. And the look on Brandon's face—priceless! She felt the microchip that they'd inserted grow warm. Was it releasing medicine?

The voice inside her head tried to push through, yet she could only hear a whisper. The medicine felt so *good* that it made her toes curl. It certainly took the edge off.

Heather cracked her neck. She felt good again. Something inside her clicked and she realized that she was sitting on Brandon's lap. She maneuvered her body and repositioned quickly so her legs straddled him. She moved in close to his face, making their hands move low between them.

"Brandon, I'm so happy to have your attention." Heather scooted her rear-end closer to his manhood. "I know you want me.

I know you feel me. I know you need me." She whispered as she pushed all that was her on top of him. Her vision turned red.

"You are *crazy!*" Brandon hissed.

He seemed so cute when he looked in her eyes. He'd released her hands, so she used them to get closer and play with his sexy blond hair. Her body responded to being so close to him. His smell just turned her on....

"Well, I can tell you one thing." Her voice in her ears, sounded like she was singing a little song. "I know something you don't know and it involves your daddy."

Heather kept twirling Brandon's hair and then moved to kiss his face. She thought she saw confusion on his face. But the medicine made her feel so good and the object of her affection was close that she let that pass. She closed her eyes and scooted closer. She began to kiss his face, neck and then lips.

She felt him take a deep breath. He was enjoying this, too! She opened her eyes and he'd turned his face to look towards the commotion brewing at the restroom door.

The anger raged back.

"No! No, you won't look that way!" She tried to wrench his face back to her where it belonged. "Don't you want to know what I know? Don't you want to know my secrets?"

The microchip warmed her again. *Ooh, it feels so good!*

She saw his face change. "What do you *want* Heather? What the hell do you want from me?"

"That's more like it." She hesitated, but continued, "I want you to go to the pageant with me. But to show you how much I love you, I'll tell you one secret and after the pageant, I'll give you some more, but at a very special price at a hotel."

Heather's body lit up. It felt like her passion was on fire. She remembered what it was like between her and Brandon before, and she wanted that again.

Brandon breathed deep again. "Tell me and I'll consider it."

She walked her hand up his chest and put her mouth close to his ear. "Did you know that your Daddy was a double CAGE agent? He worked for CAGE and the Revolution. That's what got your mom killed."

Heather let the information fall from her lips. He'd love her forever now. She felt so exquisite so she snuggled underneath his chin and smelled his lovely scent.

More drugs flooded her system and she felt so *good*.

Chapter 49

"I never wanted to be a double agent. It just happened."
—Todd Miller

Brandon sat in shock. Was what Heather saying true? His dad a double agent? He wanted—no *needed*—to find out more. He had to play this cool.

He scooted Heather back. "If you tell me more, I'll do what you want."

Brandon looked in Heather's drug filled eyes. She smiled at him giddy, high. "Oh, Brandon! I knew you loved me! I knew you wanted me!"

He allowed her to kiss him again, while revulsion tunneled through his stomach. He couldn't wait until his game with her was over. A part of him felt sorry for Heather. He knew she was on something, but couldn't tell what.

Whatever it is, it's definitely making her act like she's got two different personalities.

He could still hear the battle outside and he was worried about XJ. He had to get out to see what was going on. He put on a phony smile and said, "Heather, let's get out of here. I want to look good for you."

She purred. She rubbed her face in Brandon's neck and touched his chest. He was repulsed, but he didn't move. He allowed her to fondle him. He felt used and cheap, but it was what he had to do.

Heather leapt off his lap in a crackhead-like stupor. "Yes, let's go!" She yanked Brandon out of the chair and twirled around. "He loves me! He loves me! He's mine."

He looked at her with contempt. How long would he have to deal with this? At least long enough to get the information he needed.

"C'mon, sweety, let's go this way." Brandon spoke to her like she was a child. They left the office and he saw the commotion. The CAGE officers were delayed and the social workers were trying to bash the door in. But there was some sort of force field. He'd never seen anything like it.

He tried to scope out what was going on. Heather grabbed his chin—twisting it to face her. "Don't pay any attention to that. I want all your attention on me."

Brandon brought his eyes down to hers. *God, she's so irritating.* "Yeah. Sure. Let's go this way."

They turned down the hallway to exit the building. Heather sung some stupid song, and made their hands swing like they were real lovers. It was disgusting—especially with her in this druggy state.

"Do you love me? Do you love me? Do you need me?" Heather chanted over and over.

Brandon kept his eyes on Heather, but scanned the area—wishing she would shut up. They turned another corner and that's when he saw XJ and another girl in a storage closet.

Her eyes met his. He could tell that she was crushed. Heather ran her hands up his back, but he couldn't tell if she saw the girls.

Brandon had to think quick. He could feel XJ's fear and panic. He had to help her get out. When he looked down the hall, he saw Ziggy. Two front gate guards had captured him.

"D—Don't! L—Leave me alone! X—XJ!" Ziggy was yelling.

Brandon turned back to see that it was killing XJ not to be able to help Ziggy. But he knew just like they did that XJ had to get out and come back for Ziggy.

"Sir!" He shouted. "Sir, I think I saw something down that hallway! Maybe the revolutionaries are that way!"

Ziggy yelled at Brandon. "You s—s—snitch! Y-You r—rich b— bastard! N—No good—"

The CAGE Guards stunned Ziggy with a tranq gun, and carried him off. Brandon felt Heather turn.

I can't let her see XJ!

He grabbed Heather's face and pulled her close to his. XJ was peeking out the door. Their eyes met and he could see the pain on her face, as he closed his eyes and kissed Heather with everything that he had. His stomach turned, but he pushed it back down. No matter what, he had to help her get to safety.

Brandon could feel Heather's hungry response. He knew that XJ had gotten an eye full, but he hoped she'd forgive him. He hoped she still cared.

I hope she got away.

Chapter 50

"I have a dream that one day I'll break into CAGE and free my momma with the help of my cousins. They betta watch out! I'll make sure that nothing is standing. It'll all turn to dust, smoke and destruction."

—XJ Patterson

XJ slammed her hands down on the lab table, and collapsed down on the chair. She couldn't believe that she and Amber had made it out. They'd slipped out of the Regional CAGE office, while everyone was distracted, gotten into the government car and driven away.

She decided it was best to get rid of the vehicle, so they stashed it miles away and caught the bus home. Exhausted, she put her head down on the table. She could hear Amber talking to Granddad Kates. She was pretty sure that Amber had no memory of him or of being a part of the family.

The chatter between them became background sounds, as the swirl of emotions took XJ over. She had a small cyclone growing in her belly of anger, shock, and sadness. Ziggy was lost.

And what's up with Brandon sucking face with my uppity, white step sister? I feel like gagging!

Although a part of her knew that Brandon did it to save her, she still didn't like it. Jealously swirled, but she pushed it away. The life of a revolutionary was hard, and she couldn't afford to have wild emotions taking her off mission.

"You alright, doll?" Her grandfather sounded so sincere.

XJ rolled her forehead back and forth on the table. "I'll be fine. It's just been a really long day."

"I understand. I wanted you to know how proud I am of you. You've done a great job. Your mom would be proud, too. You've done something that she hasn't been able to accomplish in years."

She wanted to cry—scream. She missed her mom so much. But if her mom had been here XJ would've never been a part of this.

A tinge of sadness hit her. "I'm still not happy with this revolutionary stuff. I just wanted to be normal."

"Doll, you are anything *but* normal. Since Amber has connected with my system, and repaired some degraded cells I can remember better. And you are much, *much* more."

XJ held her head to look in Amber's direction. Amber had herself hooked into her grandfather's super-computer. "That looks so weird but cool. I guess it's the story of my life."

"You have more abilities than you know, too," Dr. Kates said. "I can't remember them all, but you are the most special of all. You're the leader or the cell that brings the three together."

XJ made an exasperated noise. "Why doesn't that make me feel better?"

She pushed the chair back making a scraping sound, and got up to talk to Amber. She bent down next to the terminal where Amber had attached herself.

"This chair and station looks like it was made for you."

Amber's eyes popped open. What a sight she was—with her brain all open and connected to the terminal like that!

XJ smiled."Hey, does that hurt at all?"

"No, actually I feel quite energized and refreshed. I feel like I've come home. A part of this technology recognizes me." Amber looked very happy in a geeky mechanical way.

"So what's happening over here?" XJ wanted to sound as normal as she could, standing next to the human technopathic changeling.

Amber's voice sounded mechanical. "I'm repairing some damaged cells, and working on that helmet you retrieved from the information hive."

She looked at Amber's face. It moved like something mechanized. "Did you get anything?"

"Y—Yes I believe that I have. Please walk over to the monitor on the far right. I've been able to extract the image as well as name of our last cousin."

XJ walked over to the monitor: a 3-D image of her last cousin swirled around in a circle.

"This is amazing!" She studied the image. "Wait—I think I know this girl! That's Whitney!"

"Whitney Nichelle Potts. Student at Central GEP High. Age 17. Hold. Extrapolating additional records. She has a history with gang violence."

XJ stopped looking at the monitor and turned towards Amber. "Okay Amber, you sound so creepy like that. More machine than human."

Amber turned her face and smiled. "Sorry. I've only been allowed to interact with machines on a limited basis, and for experimental purposes with CAGE. This is the first time that I've been free to be me and just explore a system. It might make me a little mechanical. I'll adjust."

XJ went back to study Whitney's image. "Yeah ... I remember that Whitney got put out of our high school and paneled for something. I remember liking her, but thinking she hung out with the wrong crowd. Wonder where I can find her?"

Amber's eyes closed, and she began moving as if she was in a trance. "You'll find her with gang members. They usually meet at Stone Mountain park after sunset."

XJ took a deep breath. "I never knew that Whitney and I were cousins. This sucks. Maybe I could've helped her or something."

Her grandfather walked up next to her. She could tell that he would have given her a hug, if he could. "I remember more," he said, sounding dejected. "I think we did this to protect the three of you. It was the only way."

"I figured that. It still sucks." XJ continued to look at the image and turned toward the incoming news. "Hey, turn up this second monitor."

It was Brandon with her step sister, Heather, walking on the red carpet for the Miss GEP High School Pageant. It was being televised on GEP TV's Teen Sensation.

Brandon said, *"Yes. Heather and I are together...."* He kissed Heather's temple, and XJ's stomach twisted.

"People have been speculating," he continued, *"but as you can see we're here together. So everyone can stop guessing. We're a couple."*

She watched Brandon smile for the camera, and escort a bright and happy Heather into the pageant. She squeezed her hands into fists.

She so wanted to scratch Brandon's eyeballs out! *I thought he'd kissed Heather to save me! But it looked like he really wanted that blond, pink freak.*

XJ was crushed but she sat up straight, realizing that she was a part of something bigger. She knew that she had to save her mom. She slammed one hand into the other. No matter what, she was on a mission.

And with the help of her family, she would destroy CAGE forever.

To be continued ...

The sequel to Breaking Free, Double Identity, will be released February 2013.

Biography

Alicia McCalla is a native of Detroit, Michigan who currently resides in Atlanta, Georgia. She works as a school librarian and enjoys spending time with her husband and son.

Visit Alicia at: www.aliciamccalla.com to sign-up for e-updates and sneak peeks of her upcoming novels.

CPSIA information can be obtained at www.ICGtesting.com
Printed in the USA
LVOW11s2308100814

398503LV00001B/331/P